NOW A MAJOR INTER

MARCELLO, M

Praise for 'Marcello's Date'
from German Bookshops

A beautiful story. Perfect for the summer holiday in Italy.
A. Preiss, Dussmann

A beautiful modern fairytale.
Frau Randermann, Bücherstube St. Augustin

Tremendous.
Frau Franz, Stutttgart

Enchanting
Frau Conrad, Buch Kaiser Karlsruhe

The best book I have ever read!
Frau Trois, Moby Dick, Erding

Exciting and, above all, a refreshing take on Love. Clearly written and beautiful to read.
Kurbuchhandlung S. Hofmann, Bad Reichenhall

Thank you. A small treasure in the Book Jungle.
Evelyn Fekl, Haus der Bücher Spaethe, Moers

Marcello's Date is a race against time, convention and reason. It leaves the reader both breathless and satisfied.
Barbara Methner, BH Braunbarth, Bruchsal

Very good; leaves the reader with a desire to be in Italy.
Johanna Wegschneider, Ahrenshoop

Super. Amazing what love can do.
Regina Baur, Elzach

Wonderful, cheerful and moving. Many thanks
Armin Huwald, Grüttefien, Varel

As tender and light as a summer breath.

Jacqueline Masuck, Dussmann, Berlin

Very amusingly and lovingly written.

Caroline Schwab, Hoehlsche Buchhandlung, Bad Hersfeld

A touching modern fairytale about love. A recommendation for all bookstores.

Josef Schnurrer – Buch Profil

MARCELLO'S DATE

By

Mark David Hatwood

Indepen Press

Copyright Year: 2008
Copyright Notice: by Mark David Hatwood.

All rights reserved.

First published in Great Britain by
Indepenpress Publishing Ltd
25 Eastern Place
Brighton BN2 1GJ

ISBN: 978-1-906710-38-5

This novel is a work of fiction. Names and characters are the product of the author's imagination and any resemblance to actual persons, living or dead, is entirely coincidental.

International Versions:

'Marcello und der Lauf der Liebe'
Published by: Rütten & Loening – Germany

‘ハットウッド, マーク・デイビッド’

Published by: Shogagukan – Japan

For information on the author please visit:

http://www.hatwood.com

For my beautiful Godchildren and their siblings, Timothy, Louis, James, Amy, Francesca, Charlotte, Ella, Annabella, Thomasina and my nieces, Paula and Lotti.

You are all dearly loved.

CONTENTS

Dearest Elena

Unfortunately, your grandfather and I won't be able to be with you on this, your special day. The trip would be too much for Nonno Vittoria's health, but we were keen to let you know that we will be with you in spirit for your sixteenth birthday celebrations and wish you all the happiness in the world.

I know your father is a deeply traditional man and that change is not something he embraces easily. For this reason, I am sure that he will want to follow the village tradition and, after receiving the gifts brought by your young gentlemen callers, insist on choosing your first date for you himself.

Your father may believe he can pave your future for you, but I encourage you to ultimately follow your own heart.

You and I, my dear Elena, are birds of a feather. And for that reason I know you will make the right decisions for your own future.

Stay true to your feelings and all will be well.

With all our love

Grandma

THE FEUD

The sun had just kissed the horizon on another beautiful summer's day in the breath-taking Italian coastal village of Vestana. Breaking the serene silence, a cockerel, from inside a makeshift cage in the Bellini garden, started screeching at the top of its voice, introducing the promise of a new day.

Through the upstairs window of a large russet townhouse on the tip of a hill, commanding spectacular views out across the bay, the small chubby frame of Signor Gamboccini stirred. Just as every morning for as long as he could remember, he pulled his bed covers back and stumbled over to the window, cursing to himself as he went.

'The same thing every morning...That damn bird!'

With his underpants hanging loosely around his substantial waist, he pushed the window open further and started screaming in the direction of his neighbour, Signor Bellini.

'Bellini... Bellini! That bird, she wakes me every day! *Bellini!*'

He started shaking his fist towards his rival's bedroom window, totally ignoring the spectacular sunrise breaking across the still waters beyond.

Waking with a start, Signora Gamboccini lifted her head from the pillow, her hair in disarray. She took one look at her husband's pathetic protests and pressed the tips of her fingers together, waving them silently behind his back.

'What is it with that bird?' Signor Gamboccini ranted, turning to his wife for moral support. 'Bellini... *Bellini!*'

Frustrated at the morning ritual, Signora Gamboccini let her head flop back onto the pillow. With a loud sigh, she pulled the pillow over her head in an attempt to block out the sound of her husband's protests.

'Bellini!'

* * *

Through the open bedroom window of the adjoining house, the enormous figure of Signor Bellini was fast asleep. Encased in his trademark string vest, with a mass of dark curls poking out at all angles, he was snoring heavily. Unperturbed by his rival's ranting, the butcher's huge chest rose and fell steadily in unbroken waves.

Just another usual morning in the sleepy post-war coastal village.

MARCELLO

The small bay that the people of Vestana used as a harbour was almost empty. A sprinkling of small boats that had seen better days bobbed to and fro in the water, the morning light casting haphazard patterns across their hulls. On a small fishing boat floating in the harbour was Marcello Romero, a slight, dark haired boy with huge deep brown eyes and a dark sandy complexion. He was helping his father prepare the family fishing boat for the day's trip. Pulling in a line from over the side, the water was running steadily down his arms and dripping onto his scuffed shoes and bunched-down grey socks. Vacantly, with his head tipped back and mouth agape, he was mumbling poetry to himself as he watched a pair of seagulls swoop about on the wind. The words spiralled around in his head and he snatched at combinations like a gannet.

'Your grace with the wind, like a dance, unawares...'

In the stern was his father, Francesco Romero, a rugged, attractive man in his mid forties with dark hair and a three-day beard. He pulled his head out of the engine hole, his muscular body and overalls covered in oil and grease. Taking one look at his son, he tutted to himself and shook his head. Dropping the tools onto the deck, he rubbed his hands on a piece of oily cloth and walked down towards him.

'Hey, Cello, what are you doing, uh?'

Marcello snapped out of his trance and looked back at his father shamefacedly. 'Scusi, Papa'

'You think you gonna charm the fish into my nets with your poems, uh? Snap out of it boy,' he said, snapping his fingers at his son.

Chastened, Marcello went back to pulling the rest of the ropes in as his father wandered back to the engine room. Leaning into the cockpit, Francesco test-started the engine. She fired first time with a burst of thick smoke from the engine hole. Satisfied with his repair job, Francesco looked back at his son, still dreamily pulling in the ropes. He made his way back towards the stern.

'Cello, you're a good boy, helping your Papa, but you're a dreamer.' He scuffed Marcello's hair fondly with his greasy hand. 'Your head is in the clouds the whole day, or in that book of yours.' He pointed to his son's back pocket which had a small pad of paper and a pencil sticking out of it. 'I worry, Cello. What about school? Poems never put bread in a man's mouth. Only hopes and...' Francesco stopped in mid sentence. His eyes glazed over as a painful memory creased his brow. '...and hopes burn, Cello. Believe me.'

Angry at himself, Francesco turned, threw the rag down onto the deck and started back up to the engine room. As he reached the cabin he called back to his son. 'Pull anchor, Cello. I must work.' Marcello obediently complied.

Starting the engine, Francesco steered the boat smartly off the mooring and headed out across the harbour towards the grey, stone-walled jetty. As they passed by, Marcello jumped with practised ease from the stern onto dry land. He turned back and gave his father a wave of encouragement. 'Ciao Papa. Only the big ones,' he yelled, stretching his arms out wide.

Without looking back, Francesco completed their morning ritual by lifting both his hands high the air, mimicking his son's gesture. 'Only the big ones, Cello!' he shouted over the sound of the motor as it chugged out to sea.

* * *

Marcello watched him go. He felt empathy for his father's frustration of having lost his greatest love, Marcello's own mother, after she had upped and left without warning three years previously. He could only wonder how it must feel to lose the love of your life.

Speaking of which...

Turning, he raced off up the high street, his crumpled white shirt flapping out from the back of his threadbare shorts as he went.

Passing the village square, Marcello raced past two spinsters - the Calonne Sisters. Despite the steadily rising heat of the morning, they were dressed in their customary black ankle-length dresses with white lace trimmings adorning the neck and cuffs.

'Buon giorno, Rosetta! Buon giorno, Leonora!' he shouted, as he raced past.

They turned and smiled in unison. 'Ah! Buon giorno, Marcello.'

'Slow down, slow down. Give the day a chance to break.' Leonora said, and the two of them shook their heads in amusement. 'That boy; he's always in a hurry. It's exhausting just to look at,' she added, as they watched him disappear around the bend in the road. Rosetta nodded in agreement.

* * *

Marcello arrived outside the Gamboccini house and plopped himself down onto a well-worn piece of stone wall, the shape matching exactly the seat of his shorts. He pulled out the pencil and the pad from his back pocket and flipped it open. Popping the rubber end of the pencil into his mouth, he fell into deep thought. Empathising with his father's pain, he used the sadness as a motor for his creativity. Eventually he whipped the pencil out of his mouth and started to scribble.

A sadness fills a lonely heart, unsalted dreams are left uncast, as love lies smashed on shores afar...

At that moment, a woman in her fifties tottered past in a pair of stilettos. She was wearing a pencil skirt that looked one size too small. Her stern face wore a generous amount of make-up and was topped off with a bouffant, blonde-bombshell haircut.

...Oh look, a poor-man's Lollobrigida, he thought, finishing his rhyme.

'Buon giorno, Signora Talanto,' Marcello said, stifling a giggle.

'Marcello,' Signora Talanto replied coolly without breaking her step.

Marcello smiled to himself and went back to his poem. As he did so, a beautifully presented silver Lancia drove around the corner. The driver – a man in his thirties with a white open-necked shirt and rolled-up sleeves – slowed and wound his window down.

'Hey. Ma che bella, la bionda,' he whistled, gesticulating at her with his hands. Marcello watched with amusement as Signora Talanto turned, feigned surprise and waved at him flirtatiously. And as the car drove off, he saw Signora Talanto run her hands over the seat of her tight skirt, removing an imaginary crease. She walked on with considerably more poise.

Marcello shook his head and went back to his prose. But, before he could regain his concentration, his eyes were distracted by a movement in the upstairs window of the Gamboccini house. Not wanting to miss anything from that quarter, his head snapped up in time to see the curtains move slightly. Marcello's heart almost burst with emotion as he saw Elena Gamboccini's deep brown eyes gazing down at him.

He was transfixed.

Then, in a burst of inspiration, he started scribbling into his pad; the poesy falling onto the page in a lucid flow.

The curtains move, so too my heart. A chiffoned glance, igniting trance, so truly bathed in aortic light...

'Marcello!'

'Oh no, the boys… what a desperate sight,' he muttered, characteristically bringing his creative flow to a conclusion as he saw three boys approaching from up the road.

Riccardo, Tito and Paulo were all Marcello's age. They were wearing the same grey school-uniform shorts and white shirts; although in noticeably better repair. Tito, as always, was bouncing a baseball off everything in his path and catching it with practised ease. His friends, used to finding Marcello in his favourite spot outside the Gamboccini house, shouted to him again as they neared.

'Hey, Marcello,' called Riccardo. Marcello's best friend was a tall robust boy with deep charcoal eyes and an intense ease about him.

'Your eyes so blue, your hair so gold...' Tito mocked, with his head held back and his arms held out in an overt theatrical pose. Paulo laughed in encouragement.

Marcello, unimpressed with his friend's antics, quickly slipped his notebook into his back pocket and slid off the wall. 'They're hazel, you idiot,' he muttered to himself as he made his way over to greet them. He gave them all a quick hug.

'Poetry's coming on then, Tito,' he jibed, knowing his friend's academic weakness. The others giggled.

'Sooo-reee!' Tito smarted, 'Face it, Marcello. The son of a fisherman hasn't got a hope in hell with the Gamboccini girl. You're dreaming if you think you're going to get a shot at her this weekend!'

Cringing, Marcello glanced up at the top left window to check if Elena had overheard.

'Armond's going to pull it off as always,' Paulo added, stating what they all knew to be true to date.

Riccardo, eager to keep Marcello from drowning in the cruel reality of his predicament, pushed his friend's head playfully to one side and led the four of them off down the road towards school. He watched as his friend turned and looked back up at Elena 's window in an attempt to steal one last glimpse of her. She was gone.

Without thinking, Riccardo gazed up towards Elena 's window too. Snapping out of the knee-jerk reaction, he pulled his eyes away in shame. *Watch what you're doing,* he scolded himself, *that's Marcello's girl.*

Despite his concern for his best friend's emotions, he found it difficult to repress his own pent-up feelings for Elena; the most beautiful girl in Vestana.

ARMOND

The Cessero mansion was magnificent; a grand Victorian building with ornate wrought iron balconies and lush vines cascading over the side of the house. It sat, like its inhabitants, proudly on the tip of a hill and commanded spectacular views over the beautiful Amalfi bay.

The wealthy ice cream magnate and his family were sitting together in a large dining room. The table was, as every morning, dressed for a banquet. It had an abundance of food laid out on a side table. From time to time a butler wandered into the imposing three metre high room to tend to the family's needs.

Signor Domenico Cessero – a middle aged man dressed in an impeccably ironed white shirt and grey suit trousers – was sitting at the end of a large oak dining table. He had his half-moon reading glasses propped on the end of his distinguished nose and was busy reading the newspaper. To one side of him was his wife, a frail, attractive woman in her late forties. Signora Cessero was dressed in an expensive tweed dress-suit with her hair pulled neatly back. The slight grey streaks emphasised the jet blackness of her orderly cut. As she poured coffee into an ornate porcelain cup for her son, Armond, she became aware of his right leg twitching irritably under the table. She tried a warm smile in an attempt to calm his evident frustration but, as with most mornings of late, it just seemed to stoke the fires of his impatience.

Even in his school uniform, Armond was a flawlessly dressed sixteen year old boy. His anger, like mornings, was rising steadily as he watched his mother serve his coffee. Irritated by her pseudo-calm demeanour, he snapped at her. 'Mama, hurry up. I've got to get going!'

'Sorry dear,' she replied sheepishly, handing him the cup.

Ignoring her obvious discomfort, Armond, stuffed a piece of toast into his mouth and glanced across at his father. 'Father, I thought it would be fun to take the new boat out at the weekend,' he tried, his leg twitching even faster in anticipation of his father's usual lack of response.

Signor Cessero turned a page of his newspaper, ignoring his son's attempt at conversation.

Signora Cessero seized the chance of a family conversation and nodded with encouragement. 'Yes, that would be nice, dear, wouldn't it?'

'Um?' Signor Cessero mumbled, uninterested.

'You and Armond, dear. You could go out together, just the two of you.'

Armond stopped eating and looked over to his father in expectation.

Signor Cessero dropped a corner of his newspaper. 'I haven't got time to go gallivanting around in boats,' he snapped. 'And don't talk with your mouth full, young man.' Taking a sip of espresso, his father lifted the edge of his newspaper again and, with a snap of the page, went back to reading.

Armond looked defeated. His leg came to a standstill under the table.

'Your father's got quite a lot on at the moment dear,' his mother said, apologetically before reaching over to give Armond's wrist a sympathetic squeeze.

Armond snapped his hand back. 'Tell me something new!' he barked. Still holding a piece of toast in one hand, he pushed his seat back and stormed out of the room in a huff.

'Have a lovely day at school, dear!' Signora Cessero called after him. Armond just grunted, his father hardly lifting his gaze from the newspaper as he went.

* * *

Signora Cessero let out a nervous laugh and shuffled uncomfortably in her seat, her blood pressure rising like the morning sun.

'Disgraceful manners that boy,' Signor Cessero said, giving his newspaper a flick. 'I have no idea where he gets it from. Rest assured it's not from *my* side of the family.'

'Maybe if you could just spend a little more time with him…?'

Her husband characteristically cut her off. 'A good beating is what that boy needs.' He folded his paper and dropped it onto the table. Standing, he took the last gulp of espresso and pushed his glasses into the breast pocket of his shirt. 'I shall be home late again tonight,' he informed her, matter-of-factly and without another glance her way, took his jacket from the back of the chair and started for the door.

'Alright dear, enjoy your day.'

Ignoring his wife, Signor Cessero thanked the butler with a nod and left the room, leaving his wife sitting at the table alone and noticeably brow-beaten.

She took a deep breath. Conscious of the butler's presence, she bit back the urge to scream at the top of her voice in an attempt to vent the pressure of the customary family breakfast.

SIGNOR SELINAS

Signor Selinas, headmaster at Vestana's *Gabriele-D'Annunzio High School for Boys*, was on the telephone. Wearing his traditional black school cape, he was in deep conversation with the principal at the local university.

'Yes, of course. I understand,' he said, officially. 'I shall make sure that this year's candidate prepares his essay for you tomorrow and that you receive it no later than Monday morning.' He leaned forward in his chair and added, 'Thank you again for your call. Goodbye.'

He sat back again and ran his fingers over his lips in excitement. As he watched the dust dance in the morning sunlight of his small book-lined room, he fought with his conscience; should he take the opportunity to rub his rival's face in the dirt? Losing the battle, he snapped upright and picked up the receiver once again, tapping a few times for a connection.

'Hello? Yes, I'd like Portorino 612, please.' His eyes roamed the mass of books on the shelves while he waited for the connection. 'Ah, Signor Sangorino, hello. Signor Selinas, here in Vestana. I wonder if you've heard the...'

'Yes Signor Selinas, we had our call from the university yesterday,' his arch rival boasted. 'Are you really applying again this year? I'm sorry to sound so surprised, only your past entrants have left a little to be desired, wouldn't you say?'

Signor Selinas' temper flared. It was true that his scholarship applicants over the past years had been a little weak. But one could only work with the tools at one's disposal. Signor Sangorino's entrants had managed to win the place every year for as long as he

could remember. But the fact his rival boasted about it at every given opportunity was, as Signor Selinas saw it, very bad form.

The headmaster took a deep breath. He wasn't going to let the man rile him. And anyway, he had every reason to be confident this year.

'Well, one must keep up appearances, I suppose,' he said, feigning indifference. 'But it would be a bitter blow for a school as big as yours to lose to one as small and insignificant as ours, now wouldn't it?'

'Well, I won't hold my breath, Signor Selinas. Now, was there anything else? As I'm sure you need all the time you have left to prepare your candidate for his scholarship essay.'

'Quite...' Signor Selinas snapped, '...and a good day to you, sir!' He slammed the phone down.

Wandering around his paper-filled office, he took a moment to calm his nerves. *How is it, that that man can raise the devil in me?*

Hearing the boys collecting outside in the school playground, he made his way over to the window and scanned the area, looking for his secret weapon. His eyes eventually found Marcello Romero wandering through the school gates with his three friends. The muscles in his shoulders relaxed. 'Let's just wait and see, shall we, Sangorino?'

* * *

Marcello, Riccardo and Paulo walked in through the school gates with Tito trailing, as usual, bouncing his ball off everything in his path. The baseball was his pride and joy, having been given it by an American soldier a few years before. Tito had pestered the G.I. incessantly for days and the soldier eventually gave in to his badgering as the tanks rode out of the village, marking the end of the Second World War.

Around them in the playground the usual pandemonium was ensuing. Children of all ages were screaming and running about in the enclosed area.

Marcello looked troubled. 'Listen boys, what are we going to do about Armond?'

'We could have the *family* pay him a visit?' Paulo joked and Tito bumped shoulders with him, their annoying habit of showing their appreciation to each other, which did nothing to ease Marcello's mood.

Tedious!

'Come on, guys, he's getting all the dates this year with his expensive presents and family money. How the hell are we gonna get any kind of chance with a girl if this keeps up?'

'Haven't seen you worried up until now,' said Tito.

'Because Elena… sweet, lovely Elena is coming out on Saturday!' and even Riccardo couldn't help giggle at Paulo's antics.

'And I suppose you haven't got an interest in getting a date this year then, eh?' Marcello growled.

Riccardo stepped in. 'Look, guys, we've got to face it. His family owns half the village...'

'All of it more like!'

He ignored Tito,'...and it stands to reason that the fathers in the village are gonna be choosing him as their daughters' chaperone. If nothing else, they'd be scared not to in case they lose their jobs!'

'The Cessero family don't own the Gamboccinis,' Marcello burst. 'They've got enough money of their own without having to grovel to them.'

'Yeah and that's exactly why they're not going to let the son of a fisherman get lucky either. Look, it's their only daughter. Old Gamboccini won't even let a boy be in the same *street* as her, never mind talk to her. For all we know, she could be dumb and deaf!'

'Don't think that'd bother Marcello much!' Paulo mumbled and Tito bumped shoulders again.

'Look, we've just got to go through the motions. Maybe, just maybe, we'll get a look-in somewhere,' Riccardo said.

'Yeah, with the Santini girl!' Paulo joked, putting his fingers down the back of his throat.

Marcello wasn't amused. 'So that's it, is it? That's your idea of a great summer, eh? Just let Armond get away with it.'

'Look, I like it about as much as you do,' Riccardo said. 'But facts are facts. He's one hell of a competition. And he's using all he's got.'

'He's an egomaniac,' Marcello snapped, 'and a cheap one at that. His money doesn't hide a thing. She'll see right though him.'

Tito stopped bouncing his ball. 'If that's Elena you're talking about, you can forget it. She doesn't have a say in the matter... and well you know it. Old man Gamboccini will decide who'll get her first date; just like every other father in this god-forsaken place. Even if she does think he's wrong, she won't have much say in it on Saturday.'

'You want to get her first date, Marcello?' Paulo said, mimicking an old lady. 'You better start thinking, sonny. Miracles haven't happened in this village for a very long time.'

'And a few hail-Mary's might not go amiss either,' Tito joked before going back to bouncing his ball against the school walls.

Marcello stamped. 'Damn!'

The school bell sounded and everyone in the playground ambled over to the entrance and up the steps into school. The boys followed, Marcello scuffing his heels in the dirt as he went. And as the door closed behind them, the silence returned to the village, descending upon it like a silk sheet.

THE CLASSROOM

Inside the bleak classroom, lines of old wooden desks filled the room. A large map of the world spread across the back wall and a huge blackboard framed the front. Below the blackboard was the master's desk with a few text books sitting to one side.

Marcello, Riccardo, Paulo and Tito were grouped together at the back of the classroom chatting. To their left were a row of metal framed windows that looked out onto a pathway behind the school. The rest of the boys in the classroom were clustered together in groups, talking noisily and throwing things at each other. The volume, as always, was deafening.

In the opposite corner, at the rear of the room, was Armond Cessero. He was sitting at his desk, holding audience with four other boys. They had gathered their chairs around him and were hanging on his every word, nodding and grinning in awe of his stories.

Boasting about his successes on the previous weekend's date, Armond's voice boomed out purposefully across the room. 'She wasn't gonna have any of it but, with a little Cessero sweet talk…' He shrugged and his friends fell about laughing. Leaning back in his seat, he feigned a stretch and looked across the room at his rivals. '...and the Gamboccini girl's all ripe for the picking this weekend, eh boys?' His sheep looked over at Marcello and, apelike, nodded in agreement.

'What do you think, Romero? Gonna bother turning up? You gotta give me a little competition this week. It's so easy it's getting boring.' The sheep laughed again.

'It's you who's becoming boring, Cessero.' Riccardo spat. 'Might be a few set backs this weekend, anyway. You're going to have to rely on your personality instead of your family money.'

Having stopped what they were doing to enjoy the exchange, the class laughed along with Marcello, Paulo and Tito.

Armond let his seat slip forward. 'Looks like that puts you out of the picture then, Riccardo.' Again, the sheep laughed in encouragement as Armond's self-satisfied smile burnt over his face.

Suddenly, a boy at the window turned back into the room. 'Here she is!'

A scramble ensued as the whole class rushed over to the window, desperate to get a good position. Marcello, Riccardo, Paulo and Tito reached the rear window just as the cause of the morning's customary kafuffle came into view.

In the road outside, Signor Gamboccini headed hastily up towards the *St. Mary's Catholic School for Young Ladies*, holding the hand of his beautiful daughter, Elena. She was wearing the usual blue school-uniform jacket and black pleated skirt, all perfectly presented. Her long black mane was pinned back into a ponytail, revealing her exquisite facial features and huge brown eyes. As they passed, she chanced a glance up at the school window where the rabble of boys was scrambling to get a better view.

'Whoooooaaarrrr,' they jibed in unison, some making suggestive gestures with their hands as they pushed and shoved, vying for a better view of the village beauty.

Signor Gamboccini picked up his pace, almost dragging his daughter behind him. The dust in the road kicked up under his feet as his urgency increased. The boys watched and whistled as she went, laughing exuberantly at Signor Gamboccini's expense as he mopped his bald spot with a white handkerchief. All, that is, except Marcello and Riccardo, who were standing in reverent silence.

Marcello had a glazed-over expression. Feeling mawkish, his eyes lit-up with hope as Elena looked back. Entering his own private Eden, the sound of the classroom faded into nothingness as Marcello silently slipped away.

* * *

Riccardo, too, taken by Elena's glance, allowed himself a few moments' bewitchment. Catching himself again, he glanced over to Marcello with shame, only thankful that his friend was still in a world of his own.

Before he could scold himself, the door to the classroom flew open and all the boys scrambled from the window back to their desks as their master and head teacher, Signor Selinas, burst into the room with typical vigour.

'Buon giorno, Signor Selinas,' the boys sang out obediently while scuttling for their seats.

Ignoring the usual hubbub, the teacher made his way over to his desk. Dropping a few text books onto it, he turned towards the blackboard, picked up the board rubber and, with mighty strokes, erased the previous day's markings.

As he turned back to the class, he stopped in his tracks. The sight of the lone figure standing at the window made his nerves twitch.

Feeling a piece of chalk hit him on the cheek, Marcello crashed back to reality. As he snapped his hand up to rub the spot, he noticed the sea of boys staring at him and giggling. Another piece of chalk flew past his head, just missing him, before he turned to face the source of the pellets.

'Signor Romero, for the last time, *take your seat!*' Selinas raged.

Marcello quickly sat down in his place, feeling like an idiot as his cheek started to redden from the force of the missile.

'I've just about had enough of your daydreaming,' his teacher continued. 'It's the same thing every day. You're becoming a distraction to us all, boy. Let this be the last time!'

Marcello, looking for a source of solace, glanced across at Riccardo who gave him a sympathetic smile and shrugged his shoulders. Tito and Paulo, like the rest of the boys, could only giggle behind their hands until Signor Selinas turned back to the blackboard and cut them off.

'Right, gentlemen, this morning we shall be looking at our history,'

Loud moans filled the classroom as they noisily heaved out their history text books from their lift-top desks. Ignoring their jibes, Signor Selinas turned back to the blackboard and started writing across it with large purposeful strokes.

Thinking the heat was off Marcello took a deep breath and gazed back out of the classroom window. He watched the dust trail settle as Elena and her father disappeared on up the hill. Just as he started to drift off again, a voice rang out across the classroom.

'And that includes you too, Signor Romero!' Signor Selinas said without turning back, as if he knew exactly where Marcello's mind was.

Caught again, Marcello whipped his head around and pulled his text book out of his desk. Hearing the drumming of his friend's fingers against the desktop, he could feel Riccardo's eyes burning into him. Marcello looked across and shrugged, acknowledging his mistake, but knowing he was failing miserably to reassure his best friend of any form of self-control.

THE QUANDARY

As the bell signalled the end of another day, the whole class stormed out of the classroom. Marcello, Riccardo, Paulo and Tito sallied down the corridor together as the other boys rushed past them on their way into the playground. Signor Selinas appeared at the door of the classroom.

'Er, Signor Romero? A moment of your precious time, if you please,' he said, beckoning him. Reluctantly, Marcello turned and walked back, leaving his friends standing in wait.

'The deadline for your scholarship application to the University has been moved forward.' Selinas informed him. 'We have to hand in your essay on Monday morning at the latest. So, tomorrow will be the last chance you have to do it.' Marcello tried to interrupt him but Signor Selinas closed his eyes and continued on. 'Now, although you don't have to be supervised for this exercise, I shall organise Signor Copello to sit with you in a separate room… to make sure you're not distracted.' He raised his finger in warning. 'And, as I have said, let this be the last time I catch you daydreaming, young man. I want to see some serious concentration from you. I've worked hard to get you a chance at this scholarship and I don't want it frittered away through lack of concentration. Is that clear?'

'Si, Signor. Scusi,' Marcello nodded, eager to get away from school as quickly as possible to discuss the more pressing matter of Elena Gamboccini. Without waiting to see if there was anything else, he turned and scuttled off, leaving his teacher to disappear back inside the classroom.

* * *

Riccardo had been watching their exchange whilst Tito and Paulo giggled behind their hands. As Marcello caught them up, he voiced his concern.

'Marcello, you've got to do something about your daydreaming. Selinas has got it in for you.'

'Yeah, you're walking on thin ice there, my friend!' Tito laughed, obviously enjoying the entertainment.

'Yeah, yeah, I know. Now, about Elena …' His friends groaned.

As they wandered out of school, through the school gates and made their way towards the village, Marcello and Riccardo were so deep in conversation, they failed to notice the collection of boys gathered around the village fountain. Tito and Paulo, however, never ones to miss a trick, allowed themselves to be drawn in by the unusual commotion. They left their friends to walk on and went over to see what all the fuss was about.

* * *

Five minutes later, Marcello and Riccardo arrived at the harbour wall and stepped down onto the slippery stones. They made their way over to their favourite place amongst the beached boats, still deep in conversation. It was only as Tito and Paulo called after them, as they ran precariously across the oily pebbles, that they realised they hadn't been with them.

'Marcello, Riccardo!' Tito cried, 'you missed them.'

'Who?' Marcello frowned.

'Armond. We tried to stop you.'

'What about him?' Marcello's heart had already started to anticipate the worst.

'He was there.' Paulo pointed back to the school. 'He stopped old man Gamboccini in the street and started sucking up to him.'

'Yeah and Elena was there, too,' Tito added.

Paulo frowned and turned to him. 'Was she? I didn't see her.'

Marcello's face dropped at the thought of having missed an opportunity to see Elena, even under such circumstances. Tito nodded and added. 'Yeah. You couldn't see her from where you were standing, but she was definitely there alright.' Paulo looked unconvinced. Then Tito delivered the death-blow. 'I think she even said something to Armond.'

'Oh, no!' And Marcello's world fell apart.

* * *

In such a tight-knit Catholic community, Riccardo realised what an honour it was for a young boy to even lay eyes on a girl, let alone talk to her. He gave

Tito a daggers look; his eyes telling him exactly what he'd do to him if he was lying. Tito shrugged in surrender.

'Listen, I'm sure it wasn't important. Something for his dad, probably,' Riccardo said to Marcello, but his friend was inconsolable. Marcello wandered off towards the shore-line with his head low.

Mimicking a stranglehold at Tito, Riccardo set off after him.

* * *

An hour later, Riccardo and Marcello were still sitting together on the harbour wall, enjoying the silence. They were lazily swinging their legs together and looking out at the beautiful evening sunset; the blood-red sun still warming the light evening breeze as it brushed their faces.

Breaking the silence, Riccardo turned to Marcello with a look of concern. 'Seriously Marcello, you've got to watch out for Selinas. He's using more chalk on you than the blackboard.'

'Yeah, I know. I just get... I don't know... lost sometimes.'

'You've been driving him mad for months and he's not one to give up easily. I know you've got a thing for Elena, but you've got to get it under control before he does it for you. And the last thing you need is something getting back to your dad. In the state he's in, he'll explode.'

After a moment, Marcello's thoughts turned from concerns about his father's short temper, back to Elena; his frustration for both situations churning his stomach like a Gip-knife. 'I just don't know what to do,' he confided. 'There's only two days to go and it's driving me crazy! I've got to find a way to get that date with Elena on Saturday.'

'Well you won't have any competition from Armond. As you quite rightly said, the Gamboccinis have got enough money of their own without having to grovel to the Cesseros. This is one girl who's not gonna be won over by money.' Riccardo let the thought linger. 'On the other hand, as I said, as much as I love you, boy, I can't see him letting her go to the son of a fisherman either. Not without a miracle, that is.'

Marcello fell silent, listening to the sound of the sea lapping gently against the shore as the sun dropped deeper onto the horizon, spraying a striking red hue across the still evening water.

Riccardo changed the subject. 'How is your dad these days, anyway?'

'Oh, OK. He doesn't say much… which pretty much says it all. He has a few good days from time to time but he's not like he was when mum was around.' Marcello looked down at his shoes for comfort. With all the emotion welling up inside of him of late, he wondered how it would be to have a mother to confide in; someone who would understand his emotions instead of criticising him for having them.

As if reading his thoughts, Riccardo asked, 'How about your mum? Do you hear from her much these days?'

'Not really, no. I had a card from her the other week. I managed to keep it away from Dad. It'd make him crazy if he knew about that.'

'Is she still in Milan with that tart of an artist?' Riccardo asked, unable to hold back the sound of distaste in his voice. Not one to hold his opinions back, even at the best of times, Marcello knew he found them extra rife in regard to the guy who he held responsible for ripping their lives apart, three years earlier.

'I suppose,' Marcello sniffed. 'Looks like it from the card anyway.'

Riccardo shook his head. Strange, he thought; how you could dislike someone you've never even met out of empathy for a friend. His mind then drifted to his own family and how it might be to be without the comfort of their daily presence. 'Oh damn, I've got to go! Gran's coming over for supper,' he said, springing of the wall and landing directly into the path of the stilettoed Signora Talanto.

Shrieking, she toppled back on her high-heels and nearly fell over into the road. For a moment he just stood there in shock before taking off, waving back at her apologetically. 'Scusi, Signora. Scusi!'

Signora Talanto managed to steady herself. Cursing, she brushed down her clothes and straightened her skirt in an attempt to recapture her poise. As she did so, Riccardo feigned laughter behind her back, making Marcello stifle a giggle.

Signora Talanto just stared at Marcello. Pulling himself together, he forced his face into a serious expression. She turned and started back up the high street, lifting her nose in the air and mumbling something indistinguishable about irresponsible teenagers.

Just at that moment, the Lancia swerved around the corner, just missing her by a gnat's whisker. She managed to jump to one side, but the driver leaned out of the window and gesticulated at her as he drove past. 'Veramente, che bella, la Signora, bellisima!' he teased, grinning cheekily.

Signora Talanto shook the back of her hand at him – more embarrassed at being caught off guard than being almost run down, Marcello mused. 'What's your problem?' she screamed, but the driver just gunned the car's engine and raced off up the road, laughing as he went.

Marcello watched the scene with amusement. *What an addiction it is to have our egos fed.* With that thought in his head, he slipped off the harbour wall and set off up the high street towards home.

Scuffing his feet in the dirt as he passed by the Gamboccini house moments later, he couldn't help the feeling he was missing something obvious. *There's just* got *to be a way to get that date with Elena.* He gazed up at her bedroom window, his heart nearly bursting while his head battled with its frustrations. *But what is it?*

FRIDAY

Just after sunrise on another beautiful day, Marcello was walking up from the harbour towards the Gamboccini home. With notebook in hand and schoolbook under arm he was, as always, in dreamland. The day promised to be another scorcher and the sun's heat was enticing the surrounding flora to release its aromatic scent onto the dusty morning air. In the distance, Francesco's boat was chugging out to sea. Marcello sat himself down on the familiar patch of wall under Elena's window, his glazed-over expression intensifying as his inspiration was fed. Placing his schoolbook beside him, he popped the pencil out of his mouth and started scribbling into his pad; the ideas flowing with their usual ease.

How to, my love, your father's heart?

A gift to fire our love... a spark,

Of inspiration from heaven, come...

'Cwwwoooookkkkkk!' Bellini's cockerel screamed, disturbing the silky silence of the morning air. Like clockwork, the window to the Gamboccini bedroom flew open and Signor Gamboccini waved his fist indignantly in the direction of his neighbour.

'Every morning the same thing... Bellini... *Bellini!*'

Suddenly, Marcello's head popped up from the notebook, his eyes wide with excitement. 'My God, that's it!'

He sprang off the wall. Stuffing his pencil and notepad into his back pocket, he raced off to the rear of the Bellini house. Arriving at the back door, he gazed up at the windows for a sign of life.

Nothing.

Taking the bull by the horns, Marcello walked sheepishly up to the back door and knocked. Moments later, the lights started popping on upstairs, followed by a series of monstrous thumps down a protesting wooden stairway. The booms ceased and a small light was flipped on inside the back door. Then, with a burst of air, the door sprang open.

There, filling the doorframe, stood the colossal frame of Signor Bellini. Two metres tall and 150 kilos, the giant towered over Marcello like a grizzly-bear. The anger in his eyes was intense. His gaze fell upon Marcello and, crossing his arms over his monstrous chest, squashing the mass of hair poking out through his string vest into submission, he bellowed, 'Have you any idea what time it is, Romero!'

'Scusi, Signor Bel...'

'We're not all like your family, Romero! Some of us sleep till sun-up!'

'Signor Bellini, scusi, scusi…'

'Well? What is it? You wake me so early, this better be good.'

'Signor Bellini, I was wondering… if you were in the market to sell your cockerel... what would you want for it?'

Bellini's eyes grew even wider. 'That's it? *That's it? You wake me from my bed for this?*' Without another word, the huge man grabbed the door and, as easy as a piece of balsa wood, slammed it shut in Marcello's face.

Displeased with his performance, Marcello screwed his face up and stamped his foot into the dirt. 'Damn!' He held his hand up against the side window and watched Bellini stomp his way back upstairs, the walls almost shaking under the pounding strain.

That didn't go well!

With no other alternative, Marcello pulled back from the door and sat himself down on the garden wall under Bellini's unkempt lemon tree, patiently in wait for a second chance.

* * *

An hour after enduring an endless stream of cries from Bellini's infernal cockerel and watching the morning sun poke its head over his garden wall, there was a rustle at Bellini's back door. It swung open and the giant appeared, forcing his huge frame through the comparatively small opening.

Slamming it shut, he glanced over at Marcello, growled and stormed off towards his shop in the high street. Knowing there was no other alternative, Marcello sprang to his feet and shot after him in hot pursuit.

The morning activity in the village was in full swing as businesses and shops started opening for the day's trade. Marcello caught up with Signor Bellini and slowed to walk alongside him.

'You have a problem, kid?'

'Scusi, Signor Bellini, but...'

'Scusi, scus, always with the *scusi!*'

'Scusi…' Marcello said again without thinking, making Bellini rasp and pick up his pace towards the butchery.

'Signor Bellini, I am sorry to have come to your house so early. I know now that was a mistake…' Marcello begged, almost stumbling to keep pace beside him. Without losing step, Bellini snorted and shook his head in astonishment at the boy's gall. '...but I would really like you to think about my proposition regarding the cockerel. What could I get you in exchange, Signor? Anything.'

Bellini came to a grinding halt, almost causing Marcello to walk into the back of him. 'What is it with you and this dumb cockerel, Romero?' he said, quickly changing his mind. 'Don't answer that, I'm not interested!' Without giving Marcello another chance to start talking, he headed off down the high street, leaving Marcello standing in his dust.

As he neared his shop, a couple of ladies greeted him cheerfully. 'Buon giorno, Signor Bellini.' Enraged by his encounter with Marcello, Bellini just barked at them, sending them scampering off like a pair of startled rabbits.

What are they so cheerful about?

* * *

With no other option, Marcello sat himself down on the harbour wall. He watched helplessly as Bellini pulled the shutters up on his butchery, unlocked the door and disappeared inside, unceremoniously slamming it behind him.

I've got to get that cockerel. It's my only chance.

As a few boys rushed past him on their way towards school, Marcello leaned over to catch a glimpse of the San Ginepro clock tower rising above the houses in the distance. He was just in time to see the minute hand twitch onto the eleven.

Five to nine. What am I doing? If I'm not in school today, Selinas is going to explode.

Coming to his senses, Marcello reluctantly slipped off the wall, dusted down his shorts and headed off in the direction of the schoolhouse, taking one last hopeful glance over his shoulder at the butchery as he went.

* * *

The pandemonium in the playground, as always, was intense. Riccardo and Paulo were waiting outside the school gates impatiently scanning the road for their friend. They knew something was amiss, having not seen him in his usual place outside the Gamboccini house. Tito was throwing his ball against the playground walls as Riccardo looked up nervously at the school clock. 'Nearly nine. Damn it, where the hell is he?'

'Don't know, but he'd better get a move on. Selinas will spontaneously combust if he's late today,' Paulo said, hardly overstating the situation.

Behind them, the insistent school bell started to sound, inciting the customary rumble of activity towards the school doors. Tito and Paulo followed suit. Riccardo took one last look up and down the road and then, with no other option, rushed across the playground to join the army of boys filtering into the schoolhouse. As he was ushered inside by a schoolmaster, Riccardo took one last hopeful glance over his shoulder before cursing Marcello under his breath.

Where the hell are you?

THE TRUANT

Having changed his mind about school, Marcello was racing back towards the butchery with the sound of the school bell ringing in the distance. Arriving back outside, but unsure as to his next move, he started nervously scuffing the dirt around with the toe of his ragged shoes.

What do I do? What do I do? Think!

Suddenly he stopped and turned towards the butchery. Then, changing his mind again, he took a few hesitant steps back towards the school, his mind waging an emotional battle with itself. *You're going to be fish bait for Selinas when he finds you're not there,* he thought, imagining what Riccardo would be saying at that very moment. But his heart was defiant. *Listen, Marcello. You've got no chance of a date with Elena if you can't do this deal.*

He got a few yards back towards the school and stopped. Frustrated with his indecision, he kicked a lobster pot lying by the harbour wall.

'Hey!' A fisherman's head appeared over the wall like a seaside puppet. 'Haven't you got better things to do, Marcello?'

'Oh, Scusi, Salvatore. Scusi!'

Slowly, his mind processed Salvatore's words.

'Grazie, Salvatore. You're right. I have!' and without another thought, he turned and headed back towards Bellini's shop.

Hesitating outside to build up his resolve, he threw caution to the wind and pushed open the doors to the butchery and boldly entered.

The onshore breeze lifted a billow of dust onto the air in the second of silence that followed. Then, breaking the tranquillity, muffled shouts started emanating from inside the shop.

'Signor Bellini, I only...'

'Aaaahhhhh!!!' Bellini stormed.

The doors burst open again and Marcello flew out backwards. He landed on his backside in the street and a few moments later his schoolbook followed, scuttling out into the dust. He hardly managed an intake of breath before a mangled piece of bone flew out after it, missing him by a whisker.

'And stay out!'

Bellini slammed the door shut with such force the 'Open' sign flapped about in protest and then fell from its perch.

Marcello pounded his fist into the dirt. '*Damn!*' he cried, making a scrawny dog, which had come to pay its respects to the bone, cower back in shock. He picked himself up, gathered his schoolbook and, dusting off his shorts, went back over to the harbour wall to contemplate his next move.

* * *

Back in the classroom the regular morning inferno was in full swing. Riccardo was sitting alone in his place at the back of the room, nervously playing with his fingers as the door flew open and Signor Selinas stormed in. The boys raced to their seats. 'Buon giorno, Signor Selinas,' they chanted, followed by the required reverent silence.

Without ceremony, Signor Selinas dropped his books neatly onto his desk and turned back to the blackboard. Picking up a piece of chalk from the well beside it, with large deliberate strokes he started writing the word *RESPONSIBILITY* across it.

'After dealing with the role of governments in history yesterday, this morning we shall discuss our own thoughts in connection ...to ...this ...word,' he said, theatrically dotting the three i's in rhythm with his last words. Dropping the chalk precisely back into the well, he dusted off his fingers and turned back to the boys. 'A word some of us may be alien to, eh, Signor Rom...?'

His eyes met with Marcello's empty seat.

Riccardo winced at the mention of Marcello's name and hunched his shoulders in expectation of the inevitable onslaught.

Tito and Paulo looked at each other wide eyed, making silent "O" shapes with their mouths.

Armond, stretched back, causing the front legs of his seat lift off the floor. He put his hands casually behind his head and grinned from ear to ear, obviously enjoying Riccardo's discomfort.

'And where, pray tell, is Signor Romero this morning?' The headmaster scanned the room for an answer and the boys started looking around with excitement. The teacher's eyes fell on Riccardo. 'Maybe you can enlighten us as to the whereabouts of your colleague?'

'I... I'm not sure, Signor. Maybe he's feeling a little under the weather today, sir?'

Signor Selinas looked less than convinced. 'He seemed perfectly well yesterday evening. What's wrong with him now… apart from the usual case of laziness, that is?' He held eye contact with Riccardo as the rest of the boys giggled and turned to stare at him.

Riccardo shuffled uncomfortably in his seat. 'I don't know, Signor. But I didn't see him at the harbour this morning, which is quite unusual for him.'

Armond couldn't contain himself. 'Oh, Signor, but I did. And he looked perfectly fine to me.' The whole class turned from Riccardo to him.

'Thank you, Signor Cessero, but your input was not requested.' Signor Selinas' eyes stayed glued on Riccardo. At that moment the classroom door opened and Signor Copello entered causing Signor Selinas to snap his head around. Being a new recruit to the school, Signor Copello wore his fears on his sleeve; his unfortunate stutter emphasising his every discomfort.

'Er, S,S,S,Signore Selinas. T,T,T,The Romero boy seems not to...'

'Yes, yes' Signor Selinas snapped, 'we've just established that. Step outside with me a moment.'

The noise in the classroom burst forth as the two masters stepped out into the corridor, closing the door behind them. A boy rushed over and pressed his ear up against the door. Unable to hear anything, he started waving frantically at everyone to shut up. The noise waned.

* * *

'Signor Copello, I have too much at stake today to put up with this boy's absence. I'm sorry to say you'll have to look after this rabble while I get to the bottom of this.' Without waiting to hear the teacher's protests, Signor Selinas strode off down the corridor. Signor Copello tried to stutter an objection but, by the time the words spilled out, all that remained of the head teacher's former presence was the boom of the school's solid oak door echoing up the corridor. Signor Copello sighed and turned back to the classroom door.

* * *

The boy at the door gave the class the thumbs up and scrambled back to his seat. Except for Riccardo, the whole classroom erupted into a burst of excitement. Riccardo pressed his fingers up against his temples and shook his head in despair.

'He's never done that before,' Tito mumbled to Paulo as Signor Copello re-entered the room and walked timidly over to the master's desk.

'N,N,N,Now, gentlemen. W,W,W,Where were you this morning?'

Ignoring his flaccid attempt at sounding forceful, the class rose out of their seats and scurried over to the window in the hope of getting a glimpse of their livid headmaster storming out of the school gates, his cape billowing up behind him like a ship's mainsail.

* * *

Sitting patiently on the harbour wall outside the Bellini butchery, Marcello was still scuffing the dirt around with the toe of his ragged shoes. From time to time the door to the butchery opened and closed as his customers came and went. Each time, Marcello's head popped up in the hope of catching another chance to persuade the man to part with his cockerel. But Signor Bellini was inside and the hopes of Marcello getting the date with Elena were in there with him, well and truly out of reach.

* * *

At that same moment, Signor Selinas burst out of the school doors and strode across the playground. The heat of the morning sun brought a light glow to his forehead as he paced on out into the alleyway behind the high street, taking the short cut up towards the Romero house. *How dare he ruin my chances of beating that idiot Sangorino!* His pace quickened in time to his rising anger.

A few minutes later, Signor Selinas arrived at Marcello's house. He rapped on the ill fitting door. Receiving no answer, he pressed his nose up against the windowpane in an attempt to see some movement in the dim interior. 'Marcello Romero?!'

Stepping back, he looked up at the upstairs windows. *Damn boy!* Fuming, he disappeared around the back of the building in the hope of having better luck there.

* * *

Marcello, meanwhile, was looking more and more anxious. He strode back and forth watching the customers come and go, but with still no sign of the man himself. He was just deciding it was time to come up with another plan to persuade the butcher to part with his precious bird when, suddenly, the door to the butchery burst open. This time, the huge frame of Signor Bellini burst out, carrying a small cash bag. Blinded by the intense morning sunlight, the butcher failed to see Marcello and strode off in the direction of the village. Marcello followed at a respectable distance, waiting for his chance to pounce.

Carpe diem, my friend.

He seized the moment and raced over. 'Signor Bellini, I...'

Before Marcello could reach him, Bellini threw him a warning glare. Marcello stopped dead in his tracks as Bellini turned and strode in through the front doors of the Banca di Genova, slamming the door behind him.

Damn!

Beaten again, Marcello wandered back over to the harbour wall and settled himself down, blissfully unaware of Signor Selinas' impending presence.

THE DEAL

Bellini had been so engrossed in his dealings with the bank manager that he had forgotten all about Marcello. Unwittingly, he stepped out into the sunlight with the empty money bag screwed up in his huge hands and caught sight of the pesky boy still sitting on the harbour wall. Without a breath, he set off with large strides towards his butchery.

Marcello took up chase. 'Signor Bellini, I…'

Bellini stopped dead in his tracks, dumbfounded at the boy's insistence. *'Whhhaaaatttt?'* The sound bounced off the surrounding house facades. 'What do you want from me, Romero?'

'Signor Bellini, Scusi, but your cockerel…'

In exasperation, Bellini acquiesced. 'OK, Romero. OK. Just to get you out of my hair. I give you the damn cockerel…'

* * *

Unable to believe his ears, Marcello's face lit up. He watched as Bellini's eyes squinted in thought, then a mean smile stretched across his chubby face. '...in exchange for a bottle of the sisters' liqueur. Got it? Now get out of my face!'

Turning, he strode off towards his shop, belly-laughing as he went. He entered through the front door of the butchery and slammed it shut behind him.

Marcello was dumbstruck. He stood in the middle of the street, his premature elation gone and his head dropped into his hands in desperation. 'Damn...*DAMN*!' he cursed, knowing full well the futility of his predicament.

Since 1803, the Calonne family had been producing a most celebrated liqueur in their Vestana vineyards. It was the talk of dinner tables far and wide. Over the years, the special recipe had been copied hundreds of times by many unscrupulous drinks companies, but with little success. Their failure only served to increase the popularity of the real thing.

Since the death of their brothers, however, the production process had become too much work for the two aged sisters, Leonora and Rosetta. After closing down production, they had decided not to sell the recipe for the family's heavenly elixir, despite many lucrative offers from some of the larger drinks companies. Although the bottles were now in short supply, each year, the sisters kindly donated one for the celebrations at the Vestana village fete. The remaining bottles were sold as needed by the sisters – their only source of income in their old age – and at a price... well, as Marcello was only too aware, far out of the reach of a poor fisherman's son.

How the hell am I supposed to pull that off?

He dropped his hands and lifted his head. 'Well, if you don't try...' With no other option, he headed off up the street and out of the village towards the Calonne farm.

* * *

Things back in the classroom were as riotous as ever. Signor Copello's lack of control was waning even further.

Riccardo had been staring at the corridor for over twenty minutes, biding his time. Watching Signor Copello attempt to deal with a small squabble between two boys, Riccardo seized the moment. He raised his hand whilst making his way across the classroom. 'Signor, scusi. I must use the toilet.' Before the teacher had a chance to register the request, Riccardo was out of the door and off down the corridor.

Seeing Riccardo shoot off down the corridor towards the exit, Tito looked at Paulo with dread. 'Oh, no; this is going to get messy!'

Paulo nodded in agreement as Signor Copello tried once more to regain control. 'N,N,N,Now boys ...R,R,R,Really! I...' he said, ducking as a ball of paper flew over his head, just missing him.

* * *

The school doors burst open and Riccardo sprang over the steps and onto the playground. As soon as his feet hit the dirt, he was off.

Sprinting up the high street, he passed the Bellini butchery, his eyes slowly becoming accustomed to the piercing morning sunlight. Further on, as he passed the turning leading out of town, he spotted Marcello striding purposefully on up the road in the distance. He took a quick glance to his right and left and, seeing no sign of Selinas, tore on up the road after Marcello.

* * *

Signor Selinas, at that very moment, rounded the bend in the high street. After trying every window in the Romero house, he was now beside himself. Heading back towards the village centre, he scanned every alleyway for any sign of the wretched boy. It was only for that reason that the headmaster had missed seeing Riccardo, who had been right in the middle of the junction ahead of him only seconds earlier.

* * *

Getting within ear shot, Riccardo shouted up to him. 'Marcello... *Marcello!*'

Marcello turned and carried on walking backwards up the road, allowing Riccardo to catch up.

'What the hell are you doing here?'

'I might ask you the same question. Boy, are you in trouble!' Riccardo gasped, spluttering like an old dog

Marcello looked victorious. 'I got it! It came to me this morning as I was sitting outside Elena's house.'

Riccardo took him by the shoulders and drew him to a halt. 'Marcello, do you have any idea what kind of trouble you're in?' he said, shaking him in an attempt to make him realise his predicament. 'Selinas is out looking for you. He's left Copello with the rest of us and gone off in search of you. You are in big trouble, my friend, capisce?'

Riccardo suddenly felt himself being shoved sideways as Marcello shouldered him into an alleyway.

'What the...?' Riccardo stuttered, almost falling over backwards in the process.

'Shhhhhhhh... Selinas!' Marcello whispered, holding his finger up to his lips and nodding in the direction of the harbour.

Riccardo peeked out to see their teacher at the bottom of the road, turning to look up the road in their direction. Riccardo's heart missed a beat as the master took a step as if to walk towards them. Then he turned and disappeared off down the high street and on past the bank.

Marcello and Riccardo waited in silence. After a moment, Riccardo popped his head out of the alleyway to check all was clear. As he turned back, Marcello had already stepped out into the street and was continuing on up the road. Riccardo followed.

'Marcello, what the hell is going on?'

'Look, I had to do it this morning. There was no other choice. Bellini has offered to give me the cockerel, but I've got to get something for him in exchange.'

Riccardo grabbed him, bringing them both to a standstill again. 'Just stop a second will you! What cockerel? What are you talking about?'

'This morning it came to me in a flash. That damn cockerel wakes him every morning.'

'Who?'

'Gamboccini!' Marcello calmed. 'Look, every morning Bellini's cockerel crows and drives Gamboccini crazy. I suddenly realised, if I could get it for him, he would *have* to give me the date with Elena. At least, it's my only chance. The thing is, Bellini wouldn't do the deal all morning. Now, though, he said he would.' Marcello paused. '…if I can get him a bottle of the sisters' liqueur.'

Riccardo gaped. 'The sisters' liqueur? Yeah right. And I suppose he wants it delivered by the Pope on the back of a Dodo? Marcello, you're dreaming! You think they're just gonna give you a bottle because you asked nicely? Why do you think Bellini asked for it? He knows you'll never get it.'

'Damn it, Riccardo, you don't have to state the obvious, OK? It's the only chance I've got. So unless you've got any others..?' Marcello raised an eyebrow. Getting no reply, he turned and carried on up the road.

'Look, I'm sorry. It's just that Selinas is after your neck and he's not one to give up easily. You know what he's like.'

'And what, pray tell, are *you* doing here?'

Nice.

'Don't be so damn ungrateful. You think I'm really gonna leave you to get caught?'

Marcello stopped and slowly turned, his lips pinched. Immune to his best friend's outburst, Riccardo accepted the non verbal apology and walked on with him. 'The classroom is a war zone and I managed to do a runner.

Copello will have no idea how long I'm gone, but I've got to get back before Selinas does.'

Marcello and Riccardo arrived at a rusty set of black wrought-iron gates. The metal was entwined with wild vine. Beyond them, a grand, ivy covered house looked out across rolling vineyards. It looked magical, set back behind a winding, overgrown driveway with oleander and honeysuckle lining its way. With a quick conspiratorial smile, Marcello pushed the gates open and carried on up the crunchy drive, the sound of pebbles popping beneath his feet.

Riccardo waited for a moment, admiring the view and then shouted after him. 'Good luck. I'll try and catch up with you at lunchtime to see how you got on.'

Without turning back, Marcello lifted his hand and waved a thank you. Riccardo then turned and sprinted off down the road, back towards the village, cautiously keeping an eye open for Signor Selinas as he went.

THE SISTERS

Marcello wandered up the pathway and around the central fountain which, for many years, had lain dry and overgrown. He stepped up to the wisteria lined double doors, which were attracting a hive of activity to its pungent smell, and pulled on a large ornate lever. A grand bell sounded inside the house. In an attempt to look presentable, he stood back and pulled up his socks which had gathered around his ankles. Moments later, the door creaked open.

Rosetta Calonne was dressed in her customary black dress with white embroidered trimmings on the arms and neck. She smiled sweetly, making Marcello feel like a rogue; there to cheat them out of a bottle of their precious elixir. 'Oh, Marcello, what a lovely surprise,' she said before shouting back over her shoulder into the house. 'It's the Romero boy, sister!'

'Buon giorno, sister!' Marcello said, with as much charm as he could muster.

'Come in, come in.' She gestured for him to enter the house. 'And to what do we owe this pleasure?'

Marcello stepped into the grand entranceway, the cool air making him breathe a sigh of relief. He gazed up in wonder at the ornate arched ceiling as she closed the door behind him. Without waiting for an answer, Rosetta set off down the dimly lit corridor. Marcello followed, his eyes reminding themselves of the expensive mosaic-marble floor beneath his feet.

As they headed towards a brightly lit room beyond, Marcello stared up at the familiar walls, adorned with beautiful old paintings of vineyards and portraits of family members. It had been quite a while since his last visit, which only made the reason for this one chafe harder against his conscience.

On entering the winter garden Marcello's eyes slowly got accustomed to the change in light. They fell, at last, upon the wizened old figure sitting in her usual wicker chair surrounded by a multitude of tropical flowers. Leonora Calonne was dressed exactly as her younger sister and was looking out upon the expanse of beautiful gardens and vineyards with contentment.

On Marcello's entrance, she turned in her chair and greeted him with a large, friendly smile. 'My dear boy, how nice to see you. We were just having tea. Would you care for a cup? Or maybe some homemade lemonade?' Before Marcello had a chance to reply, she looked at Rosetta and nodded. 'Yes of course he would, sister. Would you be so kind as to bring some from the pantry?'

Without saying another word, Rosetta obediently left the room, nodding to herself in agreement. Leonora patted the wicker chair beside her. 'Do come and sit down, dear.'

As Marcello sat down, there was a moment's silence while Leonora busied herself pouring the tea. Accustomed to the speed in which the Calonne sisters did everything, Marcello waited patiently as Rosetta tottered back in with a tray containing a large jug of home-made lemonade, the ice swimming invitingly around on the top.

'We don't get many visitors these days,' Leonora said, with melancholy. 'But we're always happy to see them when they come, aren't we, sister?' Again, Rosetta nodded.

Becoming impatient, Marcello placed his schoolbook onto the table and started twitching about, making irritable squeaking noises with his chair. Seemingly unperturbed, Rosetta poured the lemonade into a beautifully patterned glass as her sister continued. 'Ah, the garden looks so wonderful at this time of year, Marcello,' Leonora sat back with a dreamy expression on her face, the sort, Marcello considered, that is exclusively associated with old age and reminiscence. 'The times we used to have when the farm was working. Quite wonderful, wouldn't you agree, sister?'

Rosetta stopped pouring for a moment and followed her sister's gaze. As if seeing it for the first time, her eyes glazed over. She nodded in agreement and then resumed pouring Marcello's lemonade. 'You will be too young to remember, Marcello. Before all the unrest.' Her sister frowned with recollection.

Marcello's knee continued to bob up and down impatiently. In an attempt to break their train of thought, he picked up his glass and took a sip of the lemonade; placing it back on the table with a loud clunk. In the moment's silence that followed, he turned to Leonora. 'Sister, I was wondering...'

'How long is it now, sister?'

'Umm...' Rosetta hummed, consumed by the calculation.

'It's got to be fifteen years. Since the last production run, that is.' Leonora sighed. 'Fifteen years.'

Just as Marcello thought this might go on at infinitum, she turned to him. 'Sorry, dear, did you say something?'

Caught off guard, he stuttered, 'Err, I was wondering... if there was any way I could, err, get hold of…' *Spit it out, boy!* '…a bottle of your liqueur, sister.'

The reaction was instant. Their eyes widened in astonishment and they looked at him with incredulity. 'Err...' Rosetta muttered, anxiously.

Leonora glanced at her sister, then back at Marcello, making him feel like a villain. She sat forward in her chair and, uncharacteristically swivelled around towards him. 'Marcello, we…' she started, but Marcello was eager to assure them that he knew the ramifications of such a request.

'Sisters, I know that the bottles are in short supply. It's just that… well…'

Rosetta, who he couldn't ever recall uttering more that two syllables before, suddenly piped up. 'Marcello, we haven't produced a run for over fifteen years. The bottles that we do have left in the cellars may not outlive us! As I'm sure you know, we donate a bottle each year to the village fete,' she added, defensively. 'The remainder are our only source of income.'

As Rosetta spoke, Leonora had been watching Marcello with interest. As she finished, Leonora placed her hand gently on Marcello's bobbing knee. 'Well, *what*, Marcello?'

His knee froze. Confused by the question, he frowned.

'You were about to explain why you wanted a bottle,' she said, calmly.

'Well, you see…' He didn't know where to start.

'Yes?'

'Well, the thing is, I would very much like to escort Elena on her on her first date tomorrow.'

Leonora snatched her breath and looked over at Rosetta. 'That's the Gamboccini girl I told you about.' Her sister frowned. 'You know; the one who's been accepted by the university... much against her father's wishes, so I hear. Smart one, that.' The recollection washed over Rosetta's face. Just as

Marcello thought they were about to go off on another one of their tangents, they both turned to him with interest.

He continued. 'I know that I have little chance against Armond...' The sisters frowned, evidently only too aware of the young Cessero's reputation. '...and the rest of the boys in the village with their expensive gifts.'

'And..?' Leonora probed.

'Well, this morning, I thought of something that Elena's father might like. But the person will only give it to me in exchange for a bottle of your liqueur.'

'Who?'

Marcello frowned. *Are they listening?* 'Signor Gamboccini.'

'No, no. Who wants a bottle of our liqueur?'

'Oh, scusi. Signor Bellini.'

Leonora shook her head from side to side. 'Cretino!' Rosetta nodded in agreement. 'So let me get this straight. Signor Bellini has something you want. And the only way he'll give it to you is if you get *him* a bottle of our liqueur… something he believes you could never do, I'm sure?'

'Sì.'

She looked over at Rosetta and shook her head in disgust. Gradually, the frown on her face turned into a naughty smile. Rosetta, somehow reading her sister's thoughts, smiled back in the same way and started nodding in encouragement. Marcello felt a wave of dread wash over him as Leonora turned back to him with excitement. 'OK, Signor Romero, you have a deal. But we *too* have a small request of you.'

'Anything,' Marcello exclaimed, with relief. '…anything at all.'

'Many moons ago, during hard times, my brother had to sell a few items from the house to raise some well needed funds for the farm,' Leonora said and Marcello's worst fears rose again like bile in his throat. 'The Turkish carpet that was bought by Signora Tallocci was one of our favourites. Now, if you could persuade her to part with *that*, then we would be glad to let you have a bottle of our liqueur in exchange.'

Marcello let out a sigh and his eyes dropped to his feet. He was only too well aware of Signora Tallocci's feelings towards the sisters. Two years ago, her husband had died unexpectedly the morning after the village fete. And she had blamed the sisters' liqueur for his sudden demise.

The sisters smiled at each other, pleased with their wonderful idea, as Marcello contemplated their offer.

Well, what choice do you have? 'OK,' he blurted, 'I'll see what I can do.'

Loretta scrunched her shoulders with elation as she watched Marcello swig back the last of his lemonade, pick up his schoolbook and stand to leave. Her sister stood with him.

As a parting gesture, Leonora leaned over and took Marcello's hand. 'Good luck, my dear,' she said, with encouragement, rubbing her paper-thin skinned thumb over the back of his hand.

As Rosetta led Marcello out of the winter garden, Leonora settled back into her wicker chair, letting a warm feeling of accomplishment wash over her. 'Ah, first love,' she said with recollection, as the sound of footsteps echoing on the marble floor, faded down the long hallway.

THE CHASE

As soon as the door had closed behind him, Marcello was off, out through the gates and down the street towards the village. As he came around the bend in the road at the bottom of the village, he instinctively glanced over to his right. There, in the doorway to the Banca di Genova, was Signor Selinas, luckily in the throes of a passionate discussion with the bank manager. Marcello's mind went into overdrive. He instantly remembered the bundle of nets Salvatore was fixing earlier. Unable to stop the momentum of his legs, and praying Salvatore had gone for his usual morning's espresso, he raced up to the harbour wall and vaulted over. He had gone for coffee, but unfortunately he'd also left a sack of lead fishing-weights on top of the pile of nets. They broke Marcello's fall.

* * *

Signor Selinas and the bank manager turned at the sound of a distant grunt. Seeing nothing, they resumed their passionate gesticulations.

* * *

Marcello bit back the desire to scream. He rolled about on the nets, rubbing at the pain that was burning into the small of his back. As it subsided, he sat up and chanced a glance over the wall. He saw the bank manager wave in the direction of the road out of town. Signor Selinas thanked him and stormed off up towards the Calonne farm, passing just inches away from where Marcello was cowering behind the wall.

Ducking down, he allowed a short time for the coast to clear and then popped his head up again and scanned the road for Selinas.

Nothing.

Checking to make sure the bank manager had gone, Marcello sprang swiftly over the harbour wall and ran further along the road towards the school before peeling off into one of the village's many alleyways.

Signora Tallocci, here we come.

* * *

At the sound of the lunch bell, Signor Copello cowered behind his desk as the boys rushed out of the classroom, leaving the room in a blissful silence. Exasperated, he placed his elbows on the desktop, and let his head drop into his hands with a whimper. That had to have been the longest morning of his short career, he pondered, under the unfortunate misapprehension that the ordeal was at an end.

* * *

Having taken a long arc around the village to avoid being spotted by Selinas, Riccardo burst in through the school doors just as the lunch bell rang. Hardly breaking his stride, he turned on his heels again and sprinted back out of the doors and across the playground.

Spotting him, Tito and Paulo followed. 'Riccardo, wait!'

Riccardo glanced back over his shoulder and came to a halt, panting.

'What the hell's going on? Where were you?' Paulo asked as they reached him.

'Look, there's no time to explain. Marcello has got some crazy plan to get the date with the Gamboccini girl. And if he doesn't get any help, Selinas is going to string him up.' Riccardo started to back away. 'I'm going to try and give him a hand.'

'And do *what,* exactly?' Tito enquired.

'I don't know, but I've got to do something.' Without another word, Riccardo turned and ran off down the road.

Paulo and Tito looked at each other. In a heart beat they read each others thoughts and, with excited nods, their faces splintered into animated grins. 'OK, were in!' Paulo shouted to Riccardo and they set off after him.

* * *

In a small, cool alleyway, protected from the ever increasing heat of the day, the three boys turned a corner to see Marcello up ahead. He was just reaching up to the doorbell of a terraced house. They sprinted over to him.

'Marcello!'

Just short of pressing the button, Marcello pulled back as the boys sidled up along side him.

'What the hell's going on?' Riccardo asked.

'The sisters have gone for it.'

Riccardo looked astounded. 'What, really?'

Paulo and Tito listened to the exchange with interest. Having absolutely no idea what they were talking about, Paulo frowned at Tito. 'Gone for what?'

Tito shrugged and Paulo turned to Marcello. 'Gone for what, exactly?'

'...but they want Tallocci's Turkish carpet,' Marcello continued, ignoring Paulo's question.

'How the hell are you going to swing that? She hates the two of them.'

Tito tried his luck. 'What Turkish carpet?'

Riccardo didn't listen either. 'There's no way she's going to...'

Marcello cut him off with a warning glance.

'OK, OK. I'm sorry. If you can swing it with the Calonne sisters, I don't doubt you'll do it with Signora Tallocci. But Selinas is still on the warpath. You're going to have to watch your step.'

'I know. I nearly ran into him at the harbour,' Marcello said, rubbing his back where a small bruise was starting to rainbow. 'He's on his way up towards the sister's farm now, but I don't think he knows what's going on.'

Paulo had had it. 'He's not the only one. Now what the hell's going on?'

'Yeah!' agreed Tito.

Marcello turned back to Signora Tallocci's door. He lifted his hand up to the door bell before acknowledging his two friends' presence. 'Sorry guys, but I've got no time. Riccardo will fill you in. I'll see you later, OK?' And with no further ado, he pressed it.

* * *

Riccardo pulled Tito and Paulo to one side as Marcello tried to make himself look respectable. A few moments later, Signora Tallocci, a pretty, but tired looking woman in her mid forties, answered the door. She was dressed in a shawl and a patterned dress that had seen better days; the ensemble belying her understated beauty. Riccardo watched her expression light up on seeing his friend's crispest smile. 'Signora Tallocci, how nice to see you.'

'Oh, Marcello, it's nice to see you, too. Please, do come in.' She stepped back into the house allowing Marcello to enter. 'I'm sure you'd love some of my home-made lemonade on a day like this. So, tell me, how is your father these days?'

Riccardo smiled, respectful of his best friend's charm. *Unbelievable!*

As the Tallocci door closed, he felt Tito and Paulo's eyes burning into the back of his head. He turned. 'OK, OK.' he said and started bringing them up to date with Marcello's insane plan.

* * *

Back at the school, Signor Selinas was only half listening to the woes of his highly strung colleague. Still skulking behind the classroom desk, Signor Copello was trying his best to convince his superior of his reluctance to continue with the class. His argument fell on deaf ears. 'Well, I'm sorry Signor Copello, but it is imperative that the Romero boy gets this essay done today. I must insist that you look after the boys for a short while this afternoon while I find out where that wretched boy is... today of all days!' he added under his breath.

Without giving him another chance to whimper, the headmaster turned and stormed out of the classroom. In a gesture of warning, he raised his right hand as he passed the classroom windows. 'And don't let them take advantage of you Signor Copello,' he bellowed. 'Heavy handed now, heavy handed!'

He shook his finger to emphasise the point and, slamming the huge oak doors behind him, once again left Signor Copello in the wake of their resounding boom.

* * *

In wait outside the Tallocci house, Riccardo finished explaining Marcello's plan to Tito and Paulo. 'So, that's it. I don't quite know what he can offer Signora Tallocci, but...'

Suddenly, the door to the Tallocci house opened and out stepped Marcello. 'Grazie, Signora Tallocci. Tante grazie!'

'Prego, Marcello. And please send my regards to your father.'

* * *

As she closed the door, Marcello stepped down into the alleyway. Tito grabbed him and pulled him around the corner. 'And?'

'I've got to go over to the Pellos,'

'What… why?' Riccardo asked.

'She'll do the deal, but she wants a typewriter from them.'

'What… why?' repeated Paulo, like a scratched record.

'Does it matter?' Marcello spat, then instantly regretted his pigheadedness. 'She wants to start writing again, apparently. The Pellos bought the machine from her after her husband died. She'd decided to give up writing. Being a kind of lucky charm – having written all her other novels on it – she now wants it back. It's starting to look like this whole town needs something from someone else,' he added, half to himself. 'Look guys, I've really got to go.'

'But what about school?' Paulo said, reminding Marcello of the look on Selinas's face as he stormed up the road earlier.

'Look, Selinas has got it in for me now, anyway. But if I've got a chance of making this plan work, I'm going to try.'

'Probably wouldn't need to if you'd been at school this morning...' Tito mumbled and Riccardo thumped him across the chest, taking the wind out of him.

Marcello turned. 'What do you mean?'

Riccardo rolled his eyes.

* * *

Riccardo had only just told Tito to keep his mouth shut about that incident. Knowing he'd now have to explain, regardless of the impact it would have, Riccardo took a deep breath and tried to break the news gently.

'Old man Gamboccini was at the school this morning. He came in to talk to Selinas just before our lesson; something about Elena's place at university, or something.'

'And?' Marcello urged.

'And, nothing,' Riccardo said, trying to reassure him. 'He left Elena outside, so you wouldn't have missed much, anyway.'

How wrong could he have been.

* * *

Marcello's eyes glazed over as his mind quickly backtracked through the morning's events. Had he truly arrived late, as was his first plan, he would have walked right into her. Alone. Standing at the gates. A once in a lifetime chance meeting. To actually *talk* to her!

He was inconsolable.

'Oh, and by the way,' Riccardo said, giving Tito an icy stare. 'I spoke to my sister this morning and Elena was *not* there yesterday *as-Tito-said,*' he added, prodding Tito in the chest, but Marcello wasn't listening. Without saying another word, he turned and started shuffling off back down the alleyway.

'Listen, Marcello, I'm really sorry, but, if you're going to do this, then you're going to need back up. Let's focus on the mission at hand and forget the what ifs.' Marcello let his best friend's wise words sooth his emotions. 'And if I know Selinas, he's not going to give up until he gets you, so you're going to need rear artillery.' He felt Riccardo's arm on his shoulder. 'Come on. Let's get on with this crazy plan of yours. Keep close together and alert,' he added, turning to Tito and Paulo.

Marcello watched Riccardo squat down and take a quick look out of the alleyway into the street as Tito and Paulo nudged shoulders in excitement. Without looking back, Riccardo signalled for the others to follow and then scurried off.

Marcello watched them go. Swallowing his own self pity, he shook his head and smiled as Riccardo characteristically took control of proceedings - albeit a little over the top.

Typical.

He stepped out into the street after them.

* * *

Just as Marcello disappeared around the corner, the door to the Tallocci house opened again and Signora Tallocci stepped out. 'Marcello you've...' she started, waving Marcello's forgotten schoolbook at a small cloud of dust where the boys once were. She shrugged and, using the book as a fan, pottered back into the cool of her house, leaving the oppressive heat of the day outside.

THE CATCH

Signor Selinas strode purposefully along the high street, the wind caught in his cape doing little to cool the flow of perspiration trickling down his underarms. Having searched the top of the village, he returned to the centre, more convinced than ever that the wretched boy was there somewhere. He reached the junction by the harbour wall and stopped to take a 360 degree scan of the area.

Damn boy!

* * *

Riccardo, the self-appointed director of operations, popped his head out from the alleyway. Although they were out of sight of the rabid teacher, Selinas was dangerously close. Pulling back, he whispered instructions to the three boys.

'OK, he's down at the junction. 'There's only one way through to the Pellos' and that's down there.' He pointed over to the alleyway opposite. As Tito happened to be last in line, Riccardo chose him for the first detail. 'Tito, you've got to be the first decoy. Go back through the alley and down the street to the other side of the bank. If Selinas is still there, show yourself quickly and then run off towards school. He won't be able to make you out from that distance so hopefully he'll assume you're Marcello. Lose him and meet us back at the Pellos' in ten.'

Tito snapped a salute, 'Yes, sir!' and went sprinting off.

Wise guy.

Crouching down, Riccardo stuck his head carefully back out to watch the proceedings. He ran his fingers nervously through the dirt at his feet as he watched Selinas circle aimlessly in the middle of the high street, seemingly lost for what to do next. Suddenly, the master's head whipped round in the direction of the bank. 'Hey, Romero; *Stop Boy!*' he shouted and took off down the high street, beating away the cloak that had wrapped around his face in the hurry.

Like taking candy from a baby.

Riccardo quickly turned to the others. 'Come on!'

Sprinting across the street and down the opposite alleyway, the three of them looked over their shoulders, relishing the sight of Selinas disappearing off down the street after Tito.

* * *

The classroom was a riot zone. Signor Copello was trying to speak over the noise, having lost whatever minimal control he never really had. Armond and his sheep were standing around by the window talking. He was entertaining their simple minds with another of his alleged date successes when his attention was distracted by a movement out of the corner of his eye. Looking out across the school playground, he saw Tito sprint around the corner of the high street and off into the alleyway opposite.

'So, where did you take her?' one of his sheep said lecherously.

Armond doused his enthusiasm with an impatient hand signal. 'Shhhhh!' He started drumming his fingers on the windowsill and was astonished to see Signor Selinas come running around the corner in hot pursuit, looking completely exhausted. His schoolteacher passed the alleyway where Tito had disappeared and continued on up the street. The man looked ridiculous as he tried to strain his head to one side in an attempt to see further around the bend in the road. Looking tired and defeated, he came to a standstill and let his hands drop onto his knees, panting furiously.

What are they up to? Armond wondered, as he watched Signor Selinas straighten his back, turn and stagger off back down towards the high street with his hand pressed into the small of his back, massaging his lumber region.

* * *

Five minutes later, Tito appeared at the Pello house. He saw Riccardo and Paulo sitting outside on the wall, waiting patiently for Marcello, and raced over. They turned to see him bearing down on them with a roguish smile.

'Did you lose him?'

Tito smiled and held his hands out in front of him. 'Hey, you want a job done? Just call in the best.'

Paulo slipped off the wall and bounced shoulders with him. 'Way to go!'

'This isn't over yet,' Riccardo warned, a little too earnestly for Tito and Paulo's liking and as he turned back towards the door, they giggled playfully to themselves.

* * *

At that moment, the front door to the Pello house opened and Marcello stepped out into the sunlight. '...and good luck to you, my dear,' Signora Pello finished, closing the door.

Marcello made his way over to the boys with a noticeable trudge in his step.

'And?' Riccardo demanded.

'This is never ending.'

'Don't tell us,' Tito said. 'You can have the typewriter, but you've got to get the Mona Lisa in exchange.'

'Close. She wants the espresso machine from Gianni's bar.' And as soon as it appeared, the smile on Tito's lips melted.

'Damn!' Riccardo exclaimed. Seeing the despondency in his friend's eyes, he took a deep breath and looked back at all of them with resolve. 'OK, step by step. We'd better get on with it then. Come on.'

Riccardo grabbed Marcello's arm and set off down the alleyway with Tito and Paulo in tow.

* * *

By this time, Signor Selinas had returned to the high street and was standing outside the delicatessen. Desperate to find information on the whereabouts of his prey, he was deep in conversation with the local greengrocer, Signor Velta. Unluckily for the teacher, their discussion was so intense that they failed to notice the truants behind them running from one alleyway to another.

* * *

As they raced on through the shaded alleyway towards the café, Tito shouted up to the boys in front. 'Hey, guys. Did you see him?'

'Who?' Riccardo called over his shoulder.

'Selinas; we just missed him.'

Riccardo and Marcello came to a sudden halt, making Paulo, who had turned to look at Tito, nearly run into the back of them.

Riccardo thought for a second. 'OK, we're going to have to get organised. Where was he?'

'Outside the deli, talking to Velta.'

'Look, we've got to assume he's making allies. Sooner or later he's going to catch up with us, especially if we keep running about like this. Tito, you take the top end of the village, Paulo, the bottom. If you see Selinas, keep your distance. With any luck, in your school uniforms, he'll think you're Marcello. Otherwise try and keep out of sight so no one else can recognise you.' They both nodded.

'So, what are *you* two going to do?' asked Tito, slowly becoming bored of Riccardo's orders.

'I'll stick with Marcello and fend off anyone who comes too close. That way, at least Marcello has a chance of completing the mission, OK?'

Despite his reticence at being ordered around, and aware he didn't have a better plan, he acquiesced. 'Jawohl!'

Seemingly, his sarcasm was lost on Riccardo. 'Right, let's get on with it!'

The boys split up; Tito and Paulo went back the way they came and Riccardo and Marcello continued on up the alleyway to Gianni's Bar.

* * *

Not five minutes later, Paulo was jogging down an alleyway, lost in his own world. He was just starting to wonder why he needed to run at all, when he raced out of a side alley and directly into the path of Signor Selinas. Rapidly backtracking, Paulo tried to change direction; but to no avail.

* * *

Signor Selinas turned in time to see one of his boys coming out of the alleyway ahead. The boy slid in the dusty road outside Zia Lucrezias tobacco shop, the sound of his yelp as he grazed his knee on the gravel, made the man wince.

Taking his chance, he shot off after him as the boy picked himself up off the road and started darting off. 'Stop, boy!'

* * *

'Damn! Great start,' Paulo cursed, ignoring the pain in his knee as he ran off as fast as his feet would carry him. He was so close, he could almost feel the breath of his fuming headmaster scorching the back of his neck. 'Hey! Stop boy... *Stop, I say!*'

Paulo peeled off down another alleyway.

* * *

Racing off after Paulo, Signor Selinas heard the familiar sound of Luigi Callori's war-issue BMW motorbike – rescued and lovingly restored to full health by the motorbike fanatic after finding it in a farm field at the end of the war. Like a vision from the Gods, Signor Callori careered around the corner and started accelerating on up the road towards the headmaster.

Smiling to himself, Signor Selinas slowed. *Game on!*

* * *

Paulo ran on down the alleyway. Feeling he'd made some ground between him and his assailant, he looked back to check for any sign of him. The momentary lapse of concentration, however, wasn't timely. Running blindly out into the road ahead, he sprinted directly into the path of Tito.

Colliding painfully, their limbs flew in all directions in an attempt to stay upright.

'What the hell are *you* doing here?' Paulo cursed, as they scrambled to find their feet.

'I've got to run somewhere! And anyway, *I'm* supposed to be at the top end of the village, not you.'

Paulo checked his limbs for any more damage and dusted himself off. As he looked back up at Tito, however, he saw an expression of dread. Only then did he recognise the sound of a powerful engine nearing. Paulo barely had time to frown before Luigi Callori's mighty vehicle tore around the bend in the road behind him.

In unison, the boys' mouths dropped open as they took in the astonishing vision heading towards them at breakneck speed.

Signor Callori, dressed in his customary brown motorcycle leathers and matching helmet and glasses, had his head down in the wind. His wrist was twisted painfully back at full throttle. Even through his guise, Paulo saw the look of determination in his bespectacled eyes. But that wasn't the half of it. Riding pillion was their headmaster. His head was poked out from behind the rider and, with his cape flapping behind him in the wind; he looked like something from one of Tito's super hero comic books.

Suddenly, Signor Selinas' arm shot out, signalling to Luigi like a jouster on horseback as the bike fired on down the alleyway towards them.

Tito and Paulo gawped at the astonishing vision before coming to their senses. '*ARRRRHHHHHH!*' they screamed, before sprinting off down the alleyway, the motorcycle rapidly closing the gap between them.

* * *

Not far from their goal, Marcello and Riccardo were racing along a parallel alleyway, blissfully unaware of their friends' predicament.

'How many more of these are we going to have to do, Marcello?'

'As many as it takes.'

'If Selinas doesn't get you today, he'll be waiting for you on Monday. You know that, don't you?'

'If I get this date with Elena, he can beat me as much as he likes,' Marcello panted. 'Anyway, giving up now isn't going to save me. But it'll definitely lose me a chance at the Gamboccini house tomorrow.'

Hearing the village clock chime three times in the distance, Marcello added, 'Anyway, school's nearly over. If we can just hang on in there for another twenty minutes or so, he's bound to give up.'

* * *

Tito and Paulo reached the end of the alleyway. With no other option, they instinctively split off from each other in opposite directions.

The motorbike came to the end of the alleyway and skidded to a halt. Signor Callori revved the thunderous four-stroke two-cylinder flat-twin engine, awaiting Signor Selinas's instructions. Selinas made a snap decision. He waved his hand in the direction of Paulo and, with another burst of the engine and a spray of dust from the back wheel, they hurtled off after him.

* * *

Even with his heartbeat pounding in his ears and Riccardo's rasping breath beside him as they ran side by side down the alleyway, he could hear the sound of Callori's powerful motorbike nearing. *He's gunning it a bit,* though Marcello as they ran up to the junction in the alleyway and out into the sunlight.

Suddenly, Paulo shot across in front of them, missing them by a whisker. With only a split second to react, the boys started jumping in different directions to avoid falling over each other.

'Whoooaaaaa!!!'

Marcello made it across the junction successfully but Riccardo, who was one pace behind him, was not so lucky. Turning back, Marcello saw the extraordinary sight of Signor Selinas. He was leaning over the side of Callori's BMW, his hand out like a polo player, preparing to grab one of the boys. In the commotion, he grabbed the first thing he could lay his hands on... Riccardo.

Acting like an anchor, Riccardo brought the speeding motorbike to a precarious halt, nearly pulling his teacher off the back of the bike as it did so. Marcello watched as Paulo took off. He then looked back at Riccardo who was pulling himself up out of the dirt.

Before Signor Selinas could clamber off the motorcycle, Riccardo signalled for Marcello to scarper. For a second, Marcello stood there, not wanting to leave his friend to a fate worse than death. Then, as Riccardo reiterated his demand, Marcello waved his thanks and shot off down the road towards Gianni's bar.

* * *

'What on earth is going on here?' Selinas exclaimed. 'Just how many of you boys are out here anyway?'

Defiant, Riccardo stood in silence with his arms crossed in front of him.

Work it out for yourself, Selinas.

'Well, we shall soon find out when we get back to school and see just how many of your colleagues are absent,' Selinas barked. With that, he turned to his chauffeur. 'Grazie, Signor Callori.'

The motorcyclist nodded, a proud smile emanating from behind his guise. Starting the engine again, he revved it, dropped it into gear and accelerated off up the high street.

Grabbing Riccardo by the arm, Signor Selinas strode off in the direction of the schoolhouse, dragging his reluctant catch behind him.

* * *

Marcello's visit to Gianni's had been a short one. Not one to mince words, Gianni had been clear, 'Get me Santolini's transistor radio for this lot,' he had said, gesturing to a sorry bunch of men sitting around his fly infested barroom drinking cheap beer, 'and I'll let you have my old espresso machine.'

With such clear instructions still ringing in his ears, he walked around the corner and stepped through the rusty doors into Signor Santolini's small garage. He looked about from left to right trying to locate the village bicycle mechanic, his faced pinched at the stench of old oil.

'Signor Santolini? *Signor Santolini?*' he yelled at the top of his voice, taking into account the man's hearing difficulty. Suddenly, a toilet flushed from a back room and a stooped man wearing an oil-stained uniform appeared from a side door.

'Ah Marcello,' he said, 'do you need your bike looking at?

'Buon giorno, Signor Santolini. Err, not today, sir, no. I hope I'm not disturbing you?'

'Not at all, my boy. Come in, come in.'

Marcello smiled and walked over to stand beside him at his work bench so he could be heard clearly. 'Signor Santolini, I was just wondering…' he bellowed, pointing up to a beautiful wooden box sitting on a dusty shelf above them. '…your old radio; do you still use it?'

* * *

Signor Selinas and Riccardo entered the school gates just as the end-of-day bell started ringing inside the schoolhouse. In an attempt to make it in time, the headmaster picked up his pace. Carrying Riccardo by the scruff of his neck, he stormed towards the front doors in an attempt to get into the classroom in enough time to check for the missing boys.

Too late.

As they reached the bottom step, the doors flew open and a wall of screaming boys came pouring out. Impatient to get on with their weekend, the boys surged past them, sending them backwards in the wake. Regardless, Signor Selinas forced his way through, dragging Riccardo behind him and headed up the hallway towards the classroom.

* * *

Unlike the rest of the rabble racing past him, Armond was walking casually towards the front door, his hands stuffed lazily into the pockets of his expensive shorts and, as usual, flanked by his flock. He saw Riccardo and

Signor Selinas heading towards him and felt a warm glow of satisfaction invade his senses. He nudged his friends as they neared. 'Ah, Riccardo, what have you been up to all day with your three friends, eh? We missed you in class.'

Armond watched with amusement as Riccardo's face pinched like he'd bitten on a lemon. He opened his mouth to speak but the retort came from their headmaster.

'Like father, like son, eh, Signor Cessero? You two make malevolence an art form, boy.'

Armond's felt his face freeze with hatred. *No one scorns the Cessero name and gets away with it. Not in this town!* But as the headmaster stormed on up the corridor with Riccardo, he couldn't find the words to express his anger.

Beside him, one of the sheep started to snigger. Desperate for a victim on which to vent his frustrations, Armond slapped him around the head. 'What's so funny, uh?' he spat, pushing past him and storming off towards the school doors with the remainder of his entourage in tow.

* * *

Signor Selinas was just passing the classroom with Riccardo when he stopped dead in his tracks. Hardly able to believe his eyes, he looked in at the wretched creature, sitting alone at the master's desk.

Signor Copello was sitting, open mouthed, staring into the empty classroom.

'Signor Copello?'

Getting no reaction, Signor Selinas repeated himself with more gusto. *'Signor Copello!'*

Nothing.

Not wanting to waste any time with teachers who just weren't up to the job he was paying them for, he grabbed Riccardo again and strode off in the direction of his office. 'I shall deal with him after I get to the bottom of your escapades, my boy,' he said, exasperated.

Is there no one with any backbone in this village anymore?

THE TWIST

It was the end of a long and tiresome day. Marcello was trudging along the street, kicking stones through the dirt in front of him and gazing at his feet. The evening sunlight had seeped a blood orange wash into the dusty clouds, but the spectacle was lost on him. Dragging himself along, he was busy wallowing in a dusty cloud of self-pity.

* * *

Sitting alone on the harbour wall – and in considerably more physical pain than his friend – was Riccardo. His upper thighs were perched on his hands, allowing his smarting bottom to hang uncomfortably over the edge of the wall. Riccardo saw Marcello come round the corner at the bottom of the high street and, seeing his friend's tortured expression, he called him over.

'And?' Marcello asked with concern as he sidled up to him.

'Well, apart from a damn sore backside and a lot of lines, I'll survive. Rest assured you'll know how I'm feeling on Monday.'

Marcello jumped up onto the wall beside him. 'And what about Tito and Paulo?'

'We got back too late, so he doesn't know for sure that they weren't there, no thanks to that idiot Cessero, though,' he added with distaste. 'Anyway, I'm pretty sure Copello won't remember what went on.' He smiled at the memory of the man sat drooping at the classroom desk. 'I'm pretty sure they're safe.'

He turned to Marcello. 'So, out with it; how's our sweet-talking Romeo getting on?'

'It's all over,' Marcello said, dropping his eyes to gaze at the road.

'What! What do you mean, "*It's all over*"? I haven't given up my afternoon and a couple of layers of skin off my backside for nothing. Why, exactly?'

'The whole story?'

'Prego.'

'OK.' Marcello took a deep breath. 'Well, Santolini wanted a little statue from Signora Cesari; apparently he's building a decorative waterfall, or something. That was easy as they only live a couple of doors down from each other. Cesari wanted back an old flintlock pistol that he let Tomasso Manfredi have a few years ago. Why? Just don't ask! Tomasso, luckily, had no interest in it any more but did want one of Ricaldi's precious vines. Ricaldi's wife just happens to want one of Signora Remora's budgerigars for her birthday next week, so he was pleased to offer me one of his vines if I could get one of those...'

This is incredible, Riccardo thought, his expression obviously belying his impatience. Marcello speeded up.

'...the Remora's wanted a transport bike from the Baluardi's. Baluardi wants a record player from the Priest; he, believe it or not, wants Signora Granduzzi to sing in the choir again. Apparently she hasn't even been to confession for months and there's a big concert coming up.'

Riccardo coughed and circled his hands in an attempt to get Marcello to cut to the chase.

'Well, you did ask! Anyway, Granduzzi says she'll sing one more time, if... and here's the crunch... if I can get a picture she modelled for which she would dearly like to have it back.'

'So?' Riccardo said, waving his hands again.

'Well, that was bought by a collector in Rome many years ago.'

Riccardo closed his eyes in frustration. 'Sorry, Marcello, but my telepathic powers are not quite what they used to be.'

'Cessero! Signor Cessero owns the painting... *Armond's father!*' he repeated, emphasising his problem. 'There's no way I'm getting anything from Armond's house, so I can forget the whole thing.'

'You're not even going to bother trying?' Riccardo snapped, not used to hearing such a defeatist attitude from his friend's lips.

'Look, I'm really sorry you got your backside whipped but, let's face it, I've reached the end of the road. There's no way that anyone in that family's going to give me anything... especially a painting!'

'Hey! You've been getting at me all afternoon for saying stuff like that... and now *you're* starting! Let me tell *you*, Marcello Romero. You're gonna go up to that damn house and ring that damn bell and ask. If they want you to run around the village the rest of your life, naked, with a carrot sticking out of your bum, you can consider it. But I have a vested interest…' he said, pointing to his backside, '…not to let you out of this without even trying. Capisce?'

'OK, OK... *Damn!*' Marcello said, with reluctance.

Satisfied, Riccardo sprang off the wall. Having forgotten his pains, he winced as he landed. 'Good, now get on with it. I've got to get back home, so let's talk tomorrow, OK?'

'OK. And thanks, Ricky.'

Without looking back, Riccardo lifted his hand in acknowledgment of his friend's gratitude.

* * *

As Riccardo slipped off, Marcello got up. With a new purpose in his step, he started on up towards the Cessero mansion on the hillside which, suddenly, didn't seem half as terrifying.

The closer he got to the house, however, the slower his pace became. *This is a waste of time. What on earth could I offer Armond; a spoilt brat who has everything that he could ever want?* Nevertheless, fulfilling his promise to Riccardo, he trudged on… if nothing else, to prove himself right.

* * *

Armond was standing at the window of his bedroom, looking out along the mountainous coastline; the view, however, couldn't be further from his mind. As he saw Marcello's approach, he smiled to himself. *There is a God after all.* Eager to find out what had been happening all day and, more to the point, what Marcello was now doing wandering up his driveway, he tore himself away from the window and raced down their huge staircase, almost landing on the reception table as he slid over the last few steps on the ornate banisters. He could hardly care less that his mother's precious vase, with its carefully constructed flower display, had nearly toppled to the floor in the rush.

* * *

Outside, Marcello reached the massive front doors. With a sigh of resolve, he lifted his hand to the doorbell. Before he'd even reached it, the door ripped opened and there, casually leaning against the door-frame, was his arch enemy; purposefully blocking any kind of view into, or out of the house. His smug grin nearly toppled Marcello's resolve on the spot.

'Ah, Signor Romero, what a pleasant surprise.'

'Armond.'

'And to what do we owe the pleasure of your company this evening?'

Taking a deep breath, Marcello looked up at his self-satisfied features. 'Well, a friend of mine is interested in the painting that your father has in his study and I was wondering...'

'Woooow, woooow...' he said, holding out his hands. '…hold on a minute, Romero. I want to know *exactly* what's been going on this afternoon. All of it. And you can start at the beginning.'

Realising the futility of the situation, Marcello turned to leave. 'Look, maybe this isn't a good idea.'

'Hey, you want something from me and I want something from you. So spit it out Romero. What's going on..?'

Marcello stopped. *That is why you're here after all; carpe diem, my friend.*

'…and don't leave out any of the juicy bits either. Why weren't you at school today?'

OK. One more try.

He turned back. 'Fine. It's no secret to you that I'd like to get the date with Elena tomorrow?'

'Forget it, Romero, you're dreaming!'

'Look, do you want to hear this, or not?'

'OK, OK, but keep your voice down!' he said, apprehensively looking back into the house.

'So, anyway, I had this idea… a gift, for old man Gamboccini.'

'What gift?'

'A cockerel.'

'*A cockerel?*' Armond snorted, laughing wildly in Marcello's face.

'Yes, it's owned by Bellini,' Marcello snapped. 'And it's been waking him up every day now for months. So I thought, if I could get it for him, he might choose me tomorrow night.'

'Stupido, Romero! A damn cockerel?' Armond was obviously enjoying himself. 'Go on.'

'Well, he would only give it to me if I could get something for him.'

'Namely?'

'A bottle of the sisters' liqueur.'

As the words fell from Marcello's lips, Armond's mouth buckled in disbelief. 'Yeah, and I suppose he wants it delivered by the Pope, on the back of a...'

'They agreed,' Marcello said, proudly, for the first time realising the extent of his own achievements.

'What? The sisters will give you a bottle of their liqueur?' For a moment Armond's face took on an expression of respect.

'Yeah. The thing is, in exchange *they* want a Turkish carpet from the Tallocci house...'

Once again, Armond's mouth dropped open. 'Don't tell me you swung that one. She blames them for the death...'

'Well, I did. It turns out *she* wants an old typewriter from the Pellos, to start writing again or something. And they want something from Gianni and so on.'

'So you want my father's painting as an exchange?'

Marcello nodded.

'For whom?'

'I can't tell you.'

Armond crossed his arms. 'Hey, I said don't leave anything out!'

'Look, I can't tell you, OK. And what does it matter anyway?' Marcello pleaded, recalling the sensitive conversation he had with Signora Granduzzi not an hour earlier.

As a young model, she had been on an assignment in Rome where she'd fallen for a charming and talented up-and-coming artist. He had persuaded her to pose naked for him; assuring her it was for his own private collection. Years later, she had married a local dignitary and all that had been forgotten. That was until she was at a dinner party at the Cessero house the previous summer. During the customary tour of his newest art collection, Signor Cessero had proudly revealed that exact painting. 'You just wouldn't believe the embarrassment, Marcello,' she had confessed. And even though no one seemed to recognise the model, she felt it only a question of time before someone in the village would put two and two together. 'No, Marcello, I must have it back… and no one must know. Do you promise?'

Sworn to secrecy, Marcello's lips were sealed.

* * *

Armond realised the power he was wielding over his love-sick rival and he was enjoying every minute of it. Uninterested in the reason why Signora Granduzzi wanted a stupid painting, he had more pressing questions. 'So, what was going on with Riccardo and those other *friends* of yours?'

'They were helping me out. Fending off Selinas while I was going from house to house.'

Hmm. Armond took a moment to let the scenario drift through his mind. *My father doesn't like Gamboccini and Gamboccini doesn't like him. Doing a deal here might be prudent. If he does get the girl... which, frankly, is unlikely... I'll lose out. And the thought of losing to that!* he mused, watching Marcello scrape his ragged shoes around on the gravel driveway. *No way..*

Suddenly, a light went on in his head. *Brilliant!*

'OK, Romero, here's the deal. I'll give you the painting. But if this ridiculous plan does work out, you've got to let me have the Gamboccini girl!'

'What?' Marcello spurted, in disbelief.

'…the Gamboccini girl. She's mine!'

'And how, *pray tell*, am I supposed to do that? Even if I *did* agree to do it, I can't see old man Gamboccini letting someone else walk off with his daughter after he's made his decision.'

Armond saw the problem. 'No, true.' It only took a split second. 'OK. You take her down to Gianni's Bar, sit her down and then get lost.'

'Forget it, why should I?'

'Take it or leave it, Romero. It's that or nothing. And look on the bright side, you'll even get to walk into town with her!'

Almond smiled. *Talk about covering all the posts!.*

* * *

What the hell am I doing here even talking to this idiot? Marcello thought.

Whatever hope he had held onto on his slow trudge up to Almond's door, was now well and truly dilapidated.

Armond shrugged his shoulders and stepped back inside the house. 'Suit yourself. Call it a favour from an old school friend. But as the big day's tomorrow, I wouldn't leave it too long to decide if I were you.' He grabbed the door. 'Unless you've got a backup plan, that is?'

Without waiting for an answer, Armond slammed the door shut in Marcello's face.

Marcello closed his eyes, completely exhausted. *Well, like I said, Riccardo... useless!*

He turned and wandered off back around the fountain and out of the gates towards the village. The evening sun hanging by its fingertips on the horizon, framed him like a bloody backdrop as he headed off home. Beaten for the second time in one day, he was totally unaware of the reception that awaited him on his return from the wars.

FRANCESCO ROMERO

The small living room in the Romero house was a shadow of its former self. The armchairs and sofa were threadbare and the tables and surfaces cluttered with dust covered miscellany. Adorning the walls were scenes of happier times; framed photographs of Marcello catching his first fish, flanked by his proud father; Marcello and his mother, laughing together whilst launching her namesake – Francesco's fishing boat – and various group photos of the three of them enjoying summer fishing trips together. With Francesco and Marcello gone before sun up each day and rarely back before night fall, the curtains in the room remained permanently closed. Having seen precious little sunlight for the best part of three years, the plants in the room – like Marcello's father since that fateful day – had become dull and lifeless.

Sitting in a worn armchair clutching a tumbler of red wine in his hand and a rolled up cigarette flattened between his clenched fingers, was Francesco Romero. He was still wearing the greasy overalls from his day's fishing. At the familiar sound of the latch door creaking open, his eyes whipped across the room to see his son step into the house.

* * *

Dusty and tired after his seemingly fruitless escapades, Marcello proceeded to ascend the small open stairway. With each step, the rickety stairs gave up their familiar groan. Suddenly, noticing the tell-tale line of cigarette smoke reaching steadily up from behind his father's armchair, he stopped.

'Papa, is that you?' he asked, making his way back down the stairs and into the living room. 'You gave me a fright. What are you doing up so late?'

Francesco silently gestured to the seat in front of him. As Marcello sat down, he noticed his fathers pinched expression. Feeling the muscles in his neck tense, he watched as his father's hand slowly left the tumbler of wine perched on the arm of his chair and moved up to his mouth. He took a deep draw on his roll-up.

'Cello, Signor Selinas was here earlier.'

Marcello's face dropped. *Damn!* He opened his mouth to speak. 'Papa, I...'

'Whatayado, uh?' Francesco blurted, waving his hand at his son.

'Papa...'

'You want be a fisherman the rest of your life? You go around with your head in that book, dreaming! You've got a chance, Cello. You've got a real chance! I work to make your life easy and you go from school, chasing after... God knows what! Whatayado?'

Marcello looked down at his feet with shame. 'Scusi, Papa.'

'I don't care about Selinas; I care about where you are. You chase this Gamboccini girl. You dream in that book of yours all day and night.' He pointed to Marcello's back pocket, the movement disturbing the thick, smoky air between them. 'You've got a chance I never had, Cello. Today you should be writing your essay and you throw it all away… for what? For just a girl!'

Marcello's tiredness got the better of him. 'She's not *just* a girl Papa.'

'Yes! She is *just* a girl, Marcello.' He sat forward in his chair. 'You spend your time chasing her. You give her your heart and she leaves for someone else.'

'*No! ...*'

'*Yes!* I know what I'm saying. She will break you, Cello.'

Having heard enough, Marcello stood sharply with fire in his eyes. '*NO, Papa!* Just because you had bad blood with Mama, doesn't make all women that way!'

Francesco scrambled to his feet and came face to face with Marcello. 'You watch your words, my son!'

'Papa, no! You sit here day and night. You dream *too.* About what is gone. You go on your boat to be alone. You sit here at night, seeing no one. Mama is gone, Papa. *She's gone!* And she's not coming back, doesn't matter how long you sit here!'

'No,' Francesco answered, weakly.

'Si Papa. You've got to face the truth. Yes, we had good times with mama. And we can have good times without her ... *Now!* ... *Today!* But not if you don't wake up to the truth. You cannot live in the past forever, Papa.'

Francesco turned away from his son. Marcello's anger eased as he watched his father pass a hand up to his eyes and press them back hard into their sockets in an attempt to hold back the reservoir of tears bearing down behind them. His stomach locked with sympathy and love for this beaten man.

'Papa ... I love you.' Marcello said, softly, the tears welling up in his own eyes. 'But you're wasting away here. And you're trying to control my life with your own fear. *Yes*, I have school and responsibilities, but I also have a passion. A passion that will not be controlled by you, or Selinas, or anyone. I have to decide how my life will be. If it is true that these feelings I have are only with me, then so be it. But I cannot turn away without knowing the answer, without knowing my *own* truth.' Marcello wiped his forearm across his face, removing the tears that were now pouring copiously from his eyes. He pointed at his father with resolve, although the man still couldn't meet his son's gaze. 'Selinas can beat me as much as he likes, Papa! But this *I will do*... with or without your blessing!'

Having said his piece, he turned and headed for the front door. He needed to clear his head.

'Cello, come back here!' his father cried out, but Marcello ignored his pleas. Having opened the latch door, he stepped out into the warm night air and closed it firmly behind him.

* * *

For a moment, Francesco sat motionless, staring at the wall in front of him. Slowly, the feelings he had blocked for so long started to surge up inside him. With a burst of anger, he picked up his wine beaker and threw it at tremendous velocity across the room. It hit the wall with a crash, sending a lone photograph of Marcello's mother splintering to the floor. The wine that had replaced it ran slowly down the wall like a trail of deep red blood.

* * *

Marcello sprinted on down the road towards the village, his eyes red-raw from crying. Fuelled by his anger, his exhausted body carried him instinctively on to the only place of solace he knew.

Arriving at the Gamboccini house, he sat himself down in the usual place.

The full moon shone brightly overhead, sending sparks of light dancing across the surface of the tranquil sea behind him. His heartbeat slowed and, taking in a deep lung full of air, he leaned his head back to look up at the clear stars sparkling in the darkness. At last, he exhaled.

The stress and tension in his neck eased with each exhalation and slowly, he found his thoughts clearing. In an attempt to dispel the utter confusion threatening to burst forth in his mind, he let his head drop forward and concentrated for a moment on the subtle feeling of the warm night air gently caressing his face.

Suddenly, out of the corner of his eye, he spotted a movement.

Looking up into the top left window of the Gamboccini house, he saw the curtains stir. He urged his eyes to accustom themselves to the translucent moonlight. Eventually they focused upon a pair of beautiful brown eyes looking down upon him. Without blinking, for fear of breaking the spell, Marcello's eyes met Elena's and for what seemed like an eternity, they sat there entranced in the magnetism of one another's gaze.

Whatever tensions he still had, drained as he drank in the depth of her beauty. It was only after Elena 's father was heard calling her from another room and she had pulled herself away from the window, that Marcello, enthused by the moment, started to breathe again.

He started to reason with himself.

There's only one real reason to take up Armond's offer; only one reason to follow through with this undeniably impossible scheme. It's the same reason that big game fishermen ride out the stormiest seas to win their catch... the same reason that drives mountaineers across the most unholy of terrains to reach their summit... and the only *reason any self respecting poet should ever do anything. Passion! And the fact that it is only in the doing, that we truly define who we really are.*

SATURDAY

Marcello's bedroom was in the roof of the Romero house. It was small and cluttered, with clothes scattered all over the floor. Half written poems scribbled passionately on odd pieces of paper lay strewn across his cramped and chaotic writing desk and his cupboard door was held open by an overflowing waste paper bin full of crumpled versions of the same.

Having woken late on his only free morning of the week, Marcello was frenziedly pulling on his clothes. With his still-buttoned shirt slipped neatly over his head, he reached for his shorts. Only then did he notice the pile of wrinkled clothes he had chosen to wear for the evening's event still lying on the floor. He decided he would just have to do something about them later. He picked up his socks and shoes and raced out of the bedroom, slamming the door unceremoniously behind him.

Racing down the small stairway whilst pulling on his socks, he darted across the living room and into the kitchen. Pulling the remainder of yesterday's loaf from the bread bin, he tore off a large chunk and started pushing it into his hungry mouth. It had been a whole day since his last meal and, realising he had another long one ahead of him, he grabbed what he could and then started scanning the room for something he could wash it down with.

With no time to make a fresh pot, he poured the remainder of his father's evening espresso into a cup and swigged it back. *Haute Cuisine, it is not,* he mused, but it would have to suffice.

Stuffing the rest of the bread in his mouth, he quickly pulled on his shoes whilst hopping back through the living room. He grabbed the front door handle, snapped the old latch up and, to its familiar squeak, was hit by a burst of harsh morning sunlight as it opened. He kicked his heel into the second shoe, felt for the latch again and pulled the door firmly shut behind him.

With no time to waste, he sprinted off towards the village, doing his best not to choke on the dry bread in his saliva parched mouth.

* * *

Upstairs, Marcello's father was in bed fast asleep. On the dressing table beside him was a half empty bottle of cheap Chianti and a framed photograph of Marcello being held by his beautiful mother.

The sound of Marcello's bedroom door slamming shut followed by a burst of frantic steps on their wooden stairway, had woken him with a start. Before his consciousness had had a chance to register what was happening, Marcello had already left the house, slamming the front door behind him with a resounding crash.

Francesco tried to turn his head in the direction of the sound, but the sudden movement was too much. Clasping a hand to his head, he let out a low groan as the pain of a hangover bit across his forehead. Allowing the throbbing to ease, he looked over at the photograph of Catarina and his son on the dressing table. He took a deep breath and stared at it for a moment, reliving Marcello's words; words laced with a truth that had scorched him so deeply the night before.

He reached over and picked up the photograph, allowing an all too familiar sadness to invade his body. He could still remember when the photo was taken. How many times had he relived that wonderful moment and a thousand others like it over the last three years? And how many more times must he relive them again before realising the pointlessness of his hunger?

Enough!

Opening the drawer in the bedside table, he took one last look at the woman who had brought so much joy and pain to his life, and dropped the photograph face down in the drawer before pushing it firmly shut.

* * *

Marcello sprinted down through the high street, finishing off the last remnants of the bread as he went. It was another glorious day and the village activities were in full swing. The town square was packed with market stalls being constructed for the day's shopping and a few keen shoppers were already milling around, looking for some early morning bargains.

As he approached the square, a woman building a mountain of apricots on top of her stall called out a greeting to him as he flew past.

'Ah, ciao, Marcello.'

'Ciao, Signora Remora!' Marcello replied without breaking step.

'Marcello, Marcello, we see you later, uh?' another woman bellowed, winking at him knowingly as he scampered past.

'Buon giorno, Signora Ricaldi! I'll be there,' he cried, waving his hand at her.

Turning back, he just missed old Giacomo's donkey, laden full with baskets of his celebrated ciabatta. 'Scusi, Signor,' he said as he swept on up the hill towards the Cessero Villa, leaving the stall holders to chatter amongst themselves in his wake.

Minutes later, Marcello arrived at the large double doors of the Cessero mansion. He reached up and pressed the brass door bell and a warm bell-tone sounded deep inside the house. In no hurry, a maid dressed in a well pressed black dress and spotless white apron, answered the door.

'Buon giorno, Signora. Is Armond there please?' Marcello panted, looking impatiently past her into the hallway beyond.

'I think he's sleeping,' she said, formally. 'He doesn't normally like to be woken so early. But I'll check if he's awake for you if you like?'

Marcello nodded, 'Grazie.' And she went back into the house, closing the door behind her.

Stepping back from the doorway, Marcello looked up at the house in the hope of seeing some sign of life. And there, at his bedroom window, wearing a greasy smile, was Armond Cessero. Before Marcello could gesture for him to come down, he pulled his head away from the window.

Cretin!

A few moments later, Armond appeared. Dressed in his tailored nightclothes with the family crest adorning the breast pocket, Marcello thought he looked ridiculous. He was wearing a pair of leather slippers and swaggered up to the doorway as if there was all the time in the world. To Marcello's relief, however, he was holding the Granduzzi painting in his right hand.

'Ah, Marcello. Decided to take me up on my kind offer after all?' he grinned.

'Armond,' Marcello greeted him coldly.

Armond extended the painting out towards him and as Marcello reached out to take it, he snatched it back. 'Remember the deal, Romero,' he warned him. 'You don't hold to your part of the bargain, it'll be the last thing you or your father does in this village. We own you, capisce?'

'The picture,' Marcello said, simply, holding his hand out for the painting.

Armond passed it over and as he turned and started running off down the hill into the village, Marcello could almost feel the glare of contempt his spoilt rival was boring into his back.

* * *

Fifteen minutes later, on the far side of the village, Marcello was standing outside a grand house with the painting in his right hand. He had a sudden feeling of dread. Maybe Armond had played one of his practical jokes and given him the wrong painting!

Too late, the door had opened.

'Buon giorno, Signora Granduzzi,' he said, smiling politely at the middle-aged woman. 'Here is your painting.'

Her face lit up.

Without saying anything, she leaned over and took it from him, hungrily tearing at the plain paper wrapping that was protecting it from prying eyes. Turning it away from him, Marcello watched with apprehension as the last piece was pulled away and she looked down expectantly at the canvas.

The split second that followed seemed endless as she gaped at the painting. Suddenly, her stern features melted and she looked back at Marcello like a long lost son. 'My dear, dear boy. How can I ever thank you?'

Marcello smiled with relief. 'Err, church… tomorrow?' he reminded her.

'Yes, yes, of course. You can tell the priest, I shall be there.' And with a quick look down the street for prying eyes, she slipped the painting under her arm and re-entered the house.

Yes!

Marcello turned and sprinted off in the direction of the famous Santa Maria Assunta Catholic church.

* * *

Tito and Paulo were wandering along the harbour together, Tito, as usual, bouncing his ball off everything in sight. Paulo had spent the night worrying about Riccardo. His own stupidity had got Riccardo caught and he wasn't relishing the thought of hearing about what his friend had had to endure on account of his actions.

As they rounded the bend in the road, he saw Riccardo sitting by himself on the harbour wall with his head down, deep in thought. He was swinging his legs lazily backwards and forwards. 'Hey, Riccardo!' Paulo called, making him lift his head.

Riccardo acknowledged them with a wave and they made their way over to him.

'How did you get on with Selinas yesterday?'

'Oh, OK. He lectured me a bit about responsibility and the usual *"You-should-know-better-at-your-age"* stuff.'

'Did he give you something to remember him by?' Tito asked.

'Nothing that will leave any lasting scars.'

Paulo winced, almost feeling the lash of Selinas's cane against his own backside.

'I suppose we're in for the same treatment on Monday, uh?' Tito said, with dread.

'No. I think he knows you were out here but he doesn't have any concrete proof, apart from that idiot Armond, that is. Anyway, he's not unfair. As for Copello, he doesn't seem to have any idea what went on yesterday.'

Paulo aired his worries. 'Listen, Ricky, I'm really sorry about yesterday. I should have been thinking… running about like that.'

'Oh, forget it.'

Tito went back to bouncing his ball as Paulo sat down next to Riccardo, letting the silence between them express his concern.

After a while, Riccardo changed the subject. 'Have you seen Marcello this morning?'

'Not yet, no. What happened to *him* yesterday?'

'I don't know the latest. I haven't seen him yet either.'

'Selinas didn't get to him then?'

'No. He's going to be in big trouble on Monday, though, for sure.'

'And what about his scholarship essay?' Paulo asked, genuinely worried for Marcello's welfare. One thing had occurred to him the night before during his hours of contemplation; if his friend had lost his only chance of getting a scholarship because of this date with Elena, it would devastate everyone around him, including himself. If the rumour was true, Elena had even managed to secure herself a place at the University next year – a first for a girl in these parts. And anyone smart enough to do that, he couldn't imagine would waste too much time on a lovesick fisher's son. That said, Paulo's own experience with women could be written on the back of a postage stamp. Riccardo shrugged, obviously none the wiser than him, and they went back to watching Tito.

Just at that moment, Paulo saw Marcello race around the street corner carrying a metal cage wrapped in an old blanket. 'Hey, there he is... *Marcello!*'

The three of them sprang into action.

'Marcello, wait!' Paulo begged, but Marcello just looked back over his shoulder and yelled.

'Sorry guys I've got to fly. I've got a million more stops to do.'

'Marcello, hold on!' Riccardo demanded, making Marcello come to a reluctant halt. 'How did you get on last night?'

'What, at the Cessero Villa?' Marcello was bouncing impatiently from foot to foot, trying to keep up rhythm.

'What else, *dummy?*'

Paulo looked at Tito. 'Cessero villa?'

'Sorry. It's just that a lot's happened since then,' Marcello continued.

'And?'

'Look, can I fill you in later? I've really got to get going.' Marcello gestured up the road as a flutter of wings against the cage sounded underneath the blanket he was holding. Paulo was just about to tap Riccardo on the shoulder to find out what on earth they were talking about when a yellow budgerigar appeared under the blanket. Marcello anticipated their next question. 'Just don't ask.'

Riccardo pointed to the cage. 'It looks like you must have struck a deal with Armond. So, what's the story?'

'Look, sorry, Ricky, I really haven't got time to go through all this now. I've got to get all these deals done and back to the Gamboccini house by four if I'm to stand any chance at all.' And without waiting for their protests, Marcello turned and sprinted off. 'I'll fill you in on everything later,' he cried over his shoulder.

Paulo watched as he headed off up the high street and, as soon as he was out of sight, he tapped Riccardo on the shoulder, '…an explanation, maybe?'

Riccardo turned. 'What? Oh, yeah. Right, where shall I start..?'

* * *

Nearly an hour later and with the sun settling into its highest and most potent position in the skies, Marcello was tearing up another alleyway. He had an antique flint pistol tucked safely under his arm which was becoming hotter and hotter in the sweltering heat. He was only thankful that it wasn't loaded – at least he hoped it wasn't!

Arriving at a doorway to a small terraced cottage, he started knocking.

Nothing.

He tried again, this time peering in through the window by the door with his hand pressed up against the glass to block out the light.

Again, nothing.

Just as he stood back from the doorway to try and spot any movement from the upstairs windows, a small voice echoed out into the alleyway from behind him.

'Do you want to shoot my auntie?'

Turning quickly, Marcello spotted the frightened face of an angelic child gazing down at him from an upstairs window opposite.

'Oh, no, not at all,' Marcello answered, realising what he must look like; a dusty, profusely sweating boy standing in her auntie's doorway brandishing a firearm. 'Your auntie ordered it from me. Have you any idea where she is?'

The girl eyed him with suspicion for a moment. 'She went to the market,' she said, and then added; 'do you want to give it to me?'

Yeah, that would be a great idea. 'No, maybe it would be best if I went down to look for her. Thanks, anyway.'

Before he could be side tracked into a longer discussion with the girl, Marcello gave her a quick wave and sprinted off down the alleyway in the direction of the marketplace.

Two minutes later, he rounded the bend at the bottom of the high street and saw the market ahead of him. As usual, when taking this corner in the road, his eyes drifted over to look into Massimo Sorrentino's store. The small gallery's window-display invariably caught Marcello's discerning eye and usually contained a solitary *'item of the week'* in the coveted area. For the past two weeks, Marcello – along with many envious women in the village – had been treated to the sight of a most magnificent piece of finery; a vase, with an exquisitely hand-painted decoration. The piece had a small sign next to it which told of its origins and price. The potter who had made it was one of Pisa's finest and the price tag was suitably high; high enough, it would seem, to allow even the wealthiest in the small community to invest nothing more than a longing gaze as they passed.

Seeing the item gone, Marcello stopped in his tracks. Who on earth had bought it? This would surely be the talk of the village. But as he moved in towards the shop for a closer look, his heart took a leap. There, standing on one side of the counter, watching Massimo pack the resplendent article carefully into a presentation box, was Armond.

Damn! Talk about unfair play! When Mrs. Gamboccini sets her eyes on that...

With a burst of energy, Marcello tore himself away from the window. *You will not win, Cessero,* he promised himself as he raced across the road, still gripping onto the pistol like it was his life blood.

* * *

The market place was a hive of activity. The cloth covered stalls were crammed full of villagers bustling and shoving their way around the fresh produce like a flock of seagulls over a freshly gutted carcass. The atmosphere was thick with heat and the people were chattering and bargaining for the best of the day's offerings.

Marcello raced towards the market from the other side of the high street. Bobbing his head from side to side, he strained to catch a glimpse of Signora Cesari amongst the huddled mass. Seeing nothing, he started pushing his way through the crowds of women, jostling people as he went in an attempt to see around them.

'Hey, hey; watch it, Marcello,' a woman shouted as he shoved past, causing a little fruit to fall from her bag of groceries.

'Scusi, scusi, Signora,' he begged, dropping down onto one knee to pick up the stray oranges. Placing them clumsily back into the bag, he shuffled on, his haste causing more of them to drop out.

'Hey!' she cried again, as he disappeared into the thick crowd.

Having ferreted around the stuffy market stalls for a few minutes more, Marcello lost his patience. 'Signora Cesari. *Signora Cesari!*' he called out in the hope of getting her attention. But to no avail. Frustrated, he continued working his way through the busy crowd, calling her name as he went.

Suddenly, an idea struck him.

Climbing up onto the harbour wall, he used the vantage point to see over everyone's heads.

Success! There she was, in the distance, standing at Giacomo's bread stall. 'Signora Cesari. *Signora Cesari*!' he cried, frantically waving his arms around in an attempt to attract her attention.

What happened next caused Marcello's heart to freeze.

All the women at his feet suddenly let out a unified scream and dropped to their knees in panic. One or two of them started rapidly making the sign of the cross from forehead to chest. Frowning in confusion, Marcello looked around him, trying to see what the commotion was about. Following the women's frightened gaze, his eyes come to rest on his own right hand, waving the flint pistol about in the air. Realising his mistake, he quickly dropped his hand. 'Scusi, scusi,' he begged, jumping down off the wall. 'It is a gift for Signora Cesari.' Before the women understood what he was saying and had chance to wreak their vengeance, he was off. He raced through the crowd towards Signora Cesari as quickly as his legs would carry him, ignoring the rising sounds of dissent behind him.

A minute later, he sidled up to the bread stand. 'Signora Cesari, I have the pistol,' he said, with excitement. She turned and frowned. 'The flint pistol you wanted?' he reminded her, pointing at it and nodding.

Slowly her look of confusion changed and her face lit up. 'Ah, Marcello, the pistol. Sì, sì. I waited for you yesterday but you didn't come.'

'Scusi Signora, but I did say I wouldn't be able to get it until today. Can we go now?' he added, impatiently pulling on her arm.

'But my shopping...'

Ignoring her protests, Marcello started to pull her bags off her, trying to speed up her exit. 'I'll help you,' he tried, but Signora Cesari fought him off. In the scuffle, a little fruit fell out of the top of the bag and dropped onto the dusty ground. 'Scusi, scusi, Signora,' Marcello repeated, picking up the fruit and placing it hurriedly back into the bags. When the last piece of fruit was packed, Marcello tugged, gently this time, on her arm in an attempt to make her go with him.

'Marcello, I...' she tried, but Marcello's insistence was unyielding.

'This won't take a moment, Signora. Please?'

Giving in to his gentle persuasion, she followed him out of the marketplace and on up towards her house.

* * *

Less than ten minutes later, Marcello sprang off her top step and sprinted off down the alleyway carrying a small clay replica of the Venus de Milo under his arm.

'Ciao, Marcello,' Signora Cesari waved after him.

Grateful for her help, Marcello looked back to wave his goodbyes. In doing so, he broke out from the alleyway into the road looking in the wrong directing. Turning back too late, he ran straight into the stillettoed Signora Talanto who was returning home from the market with her day's shopping.

'Aaaahhhhh!' they screamed in unison as he approached at an unstoppable speed.

Marcello tried to skip around her, catching both her shopping bags as he passed. Her groceries went into an uncontrollable spin.

Losing her fight to stay upright, she fell like a drunk into the road, her shopping scattering all over the place. Marcello came to a halt, just managing to stop the clay statue from falling from of his hands. He turned back to evaluate the damage. 'Oh, scusi, scusi Signora,' he begged, seeing her dishevelled form lying in a heap in the road. Acting like a perfect gentleman, he tried to help her to her feet.

'Get away from me! *Away!*' she snapped, getting up herself.

As she did so, Marcello busied himself by gathering her shopping from the dusty road.

'Get away from that. Get away from me, and *stay away!*' she bellowed, waving a hand at him furiously. In doing so, she toppled backwards into the dirt. Angrier now, her eyes started darting about, scanning the road for something to throw at him. Grabbing the first thing to hand, she pitched a ripe tomato with all the power she could muster. Missing him by a mile, it flew past and went squelching off down the road towards the harbour like a runaway beach-ball.

'Scusi, Signora,' Marcello repeated, giving up his rejected offer of assistance. Knowing he was wasting his time persevering, he set off down the road with a look of honest sorrow. 'Mille volte scusi.'

* * *

Signora Talanto watched him go. *Aggravating child!*

Once again, she tried to get to her feet. This time, she was only half way up before the heel on her stiletto broke off. She landed back into the grit with a thud, her carefully styled hair falling to one side in disarray.

At that moment, as if by clockwork, the Lancia swiftly drove around the corner.

She couldn't believe it. *Why me!*

With a smarmy grin, the driver started waving at her, evidently enjoying the spectacle. 'Coraggio, Signora,' he shouted, with a self-satisfied chuckle. 'Mi piagge anche cosi.'

Signora Talanto boiled over. Grabbing the heel from her broken stiletto, she threw it at him. The missile whipped through the air on a perfect trajectory.

'What the..?' The driver swiftly brought his hand up to his face in self defence… but all too late.

For a split second, everything broke into slow motion. To Signor Talanto's amazement, the heel of her stiletto glided smoothly through the air, hitting the side of his smug face with a dull thud before ricocheting off. The driver screeched to a halt, in shock almost driving into the side of a building. Coming to his senses, he started wincing like a schoolboy at the slowly reddening mark growing on his cheek.

Signora Talanto stared, stunned by the perfection of the moment. Then, for the first time in what seemed like years, she felt her muscles relax as an uncontrollable belly-laugh surged up like a tidal wave through her body. Unable to contain herself, the laughter spilled forth like a dam with its banks broken.

She toppled back in the road, laughing like she hadn't done in years, the pent up tears of amusement cascading down her face like a waterfall.

* * *

With his ego in tatters, the Romeo revved his engine, slipped the car in gear and sped off down the road towards the harbour, the woman's unrestrained laughter ringing in his ears as he went.

THE PREPARATION

In an expensively decorated bedroom with gold ornaments and solid oak furniture cocooning him from the outside world, Armond was slowly laying a few items of clothing out on the four poster bed. The room was styled to his father's taste. It was yet another thing that Armond hated about his life in this house. Why he wasn't able to have the room furnished to his *own* choice of decor was beyond him. His father had no idea of the modern trends that adorned the pages of his mother's magazines and the fact that he was a prisoner of his father's antiquated tastes, even in his own room, was of constant irritation to him.

He stuck his head back into the regally carved solid-oak wardrobe and started looking around for his silk shirts, getting more and more annoyed in the process. *Nothing is ever where it should be in this godforsaken place!* Giving up, he turned towards the closed bedroom door and screamed angrily.

'Maria! ...*Ma – ri – a!*'

A few moments later there was a knock at the door and the maid stepped into the room, looking nervous and flustered. 'Sì, Signor?'

'Maria, where are my silk shirts?'

'Scusi, Signor, but they have been sent to the cleaners.'

'What! All of them?'

'Sì, Signor. Your mother, she thought you'd like it if...'

'No Maria! I don't *like it!*' he snapped. 'You know I have a date this evening at the Gamboccini house and I expect to be wearing a silk shirt for the occasion so I suggest you find one for me... *Rapido!*'

'Sì, Signor,' the maid replied, obediently and scuttled off out of the room, closing the door gently behind her.

Armond shook his head. *Incompetence!* He was about to return his attention to the wardrobe when he abruptly turned to look at the ornate clock sitting on the dressing table behind him. 'Two thirty, already. Damn woman,' he mumbled, not sure himself whether he was referring to Maria, or his own mother. Deciding to cover himself for every possible scenario, he stuck his head back into the cupboard and resumed his search for a suitable substitute.

* * *

Carrying a monster of a radio in his arms, Marcello was struggling up the high street. The village was much quieter after the end of the day's trading and behind him a few stall holders were filling their carts with the rest of the unsold produce. At last, he saw Gianni's Bar in the distance. *If I can just make it over there before my arms fall off,* he thought, urging his exhausted body on.

Moments later, he staggered over the threshold of the cafe and placed the ridiculously heavy transistor onto the floor. He breathed in the syrupy mix of tobacco and roasted coffee beans – which would forever remind him of breakfast at home – as he lumped the cumbersome box up onto his knee and then onto the bar, nearly pulling a muscle in his back in the process. 'Your radio, Gianni.'

The short balding owner came running out from the back room, almost knocking over his young waiter in the hurry. 'Marcello, Marcello!' he gasped, holding his hands up to his chubby face. Without registering Marcello's exhaustion, he started caressing the box like it was a long lost son. Eventually, he turned to Marcello. 'Grazie, Marcello. Grazie. Now, what can I get you, my boy? …anything.'

'Prego. An espresso, please, Gianni... and then the machine, if you'd be so kind.'

* * *

Looking decidedly smarter than he had in years, wearing a neatly pressed white shirt and clean denim jeans, Francesco Romero was strolling happily along the high street taking in the afternoon air. As he turned the corner, however, he stopped dead in his tracks. Across the piazza he saw his bedraggled son stagger into Gianni's bar carrying an enormous box. The boy was covered from head to toe in dust and sweat and looked like a rabid dog. Francesco's heart went out to him.

What is he up to? he mused, knowing truthfully that he was wasting his time when it came to trying to fathom the depths of his son's thinking.

Instinctively he looked up at the San Ginepro clock in the distance. *Two-thirty... I must do something. But is there still enough time?*

Pushing the thought aside, he turned and strode off towards home.

* * *

At that moment, Marcello stepped back out of the cafe doors with Gianni's espresso machine under his arm. The machine was hot and was cutting into Marcello's ribs. Nevertheless, inspired by Gianni's caffeine-rich brew, his little legs carried him off down the road and into an alleyway beyond.

The day's events had taken much longer than he'd hoped and time was no longer on his side. He sprinted as fast as he possibly could, feeling the clouds of dust billowing up behind him as he raced on to his next port of call. On reaching the end of the alleyway, he went to turn the corner and stopped dead in his tracks. There, just across the far side of the road, standing like a heavenly vision and looking directly into his eyes, was Elena Gamboccini.

She looked breathtaking.

Her simply patterned knee-length summer dress hung loosely around her slim figure. Her long, shiny, shadow-black hair hung freely behind her, glistening and swaying in the light breeze. And, as he looked into her deep honeydew eyes, he felt a waterfall of prose pour forth in his mind.

Nothing in his body would move. He stood there, transfixed, his limbs awaiting instructions from his strangled brain.

From across the road, the larger-than-life figure of Elena's mother turned to see what was going on. Wearing the traditional long black dress with crocheted white lace cuffs and collar, she had been deep in conversation with her friend until they had both stopped talking, a sixth sense making them aware of a presence behind them.

'Elena!' she barked, folding her arms over her chest in expectation of her daughter's obedient and immediate reaction. For a second, Elena ignored her, but the call was enough to break Marcello out of his trance.

'I… err...' he mumbled to Elena, stumbling over his words.

Elena's mother broke away from her friend and shadowed up behind her daughter. 'Elena?'

Her deep warning tone caused her daughter to snap her head around. Elena respectfully lowered her eyes.

Before another word could be spoken, her mother turned and started off up the road, her silent actions signalling for her daughter to follow. Elena threw one last grin at Marcello. Then, turning quickly, she dutifully followed.

Marcello's mind started to race uncontrollably. *What an idiot! That was your big chance and you blew it!* He frowned. *Wait a minute, why did she smile? Did she think I was pathetic? Maybe she just feels sorry for me?*

No time to speculate!

His limbs at last receiving instruction from his brain, he sparked into action. Heaving the machine back up under his arm, he made his way off down the road, his mind a flurry of self condemning thoughts.

"I... err..." Brilliant! You idiot!

* * *

Riccardo and Paulo were still sitting on the harbour wall watching Tito pound his ball into the buildings in front of them and catching it with professional ease. They'd been sitting there for what seemed like an age, mesmerised by Tito's monotonous rhythms. After quiet contemplation, Riccardo turned to Paulo and broke the long silence. 'I wonder how Marcello's getting on.'

'Don't know, but if he's got any chance of being there at all, he'd better get his skates on. Can't be much time left, eh?'

'Suppose not.'

Riccardo strained his head around to try and see the time. Unable to get a good look from where he was sitting, and too lazy to get up, he shouted over to Tito. 'What time is it, Tito?'

Tito threw his ball up into the air, spun around on his heels towards the San Ginepro clock tower before expertly catching the leathery sphere behind his back. 'Just gone three o'clock.' Suddenly, he stuffed the ball into his back pocket and turned to them. 'Hey, we better get going!'

Riccardo and Paulo frowned at one another.

'To get changed...' Tito continued, evidently thinking he was stating the obvious.

Hardly believing his own ears, Riccardo suddenly realised what he must be talking about. 'What! You want to go up to the Gamboccini house?'

'Yeah, why not? I've got as much chance as the next man.'

'Why not? *Why not*? Have you got nuts for brains?' Tito stood looking at him with a vague expression. Exasperated, Riccardo spelt it out for him. 'You're going to go up to the Gamboccini house and try and get the date with Elena? Don't you see a slight problem there?'

Tito frowned, his eyes rolling around in their sockets. His expression telling Riccardo he just didn't get it. 'Look, let's just say you do pull it off. How on earth are you going to explain that to Marcello, huh?'

'Well, err...'

Riccardo continued, frustrated at his friend's stupidity. 'You're happily going to take her off for the evening, knowing what that would do to Marcello... your, *so called* friend! *Are you dumb?*'

'He's right, Tito,' Paulo added, calmly. 'You can't do it... not with this girl, anyway.'

'I never really thought about it that way,' Tito mumbled.

Riccardo couldn't believe his ears. 'What do you think yesterday was all about? Just a bit of fun and games?'

Paulo, showing uncharacteristic diplomacy, turned to Riccardo and laid his hand on his friends shoulder. 'OK, OK. I think he's got it.'

Riccardo relaxed.

Reluctantly, Tito pulled the ball out of his back pocket again and went back to his favourite pastime.

After taking a moment to settle his nerves, Riccardo turned to Paulo, 'I hope he pulls it off. He's going to be impossible if he doesn't.'

'He's going to be impossible if he does!' Paulo added and they nodded in agreement at the undeniable fact before returning to the monotony of watching Tito bounce his precious baseball off the sandy brick walls in front of them.

* * *

Fifteen long minutes later, in the alleyway not far from where his friends were sitting, Marcello came struggling out of the Tallocci house with a huge Turkish carpet. Slung over his shoulder, it was balanced precariously and, in an attempt to stop the end from rubbing along behind him in the dirt, he had to lift himself up onto his toes.

From her doorstep, Signora Tallocci watched him stagger off. Suddenly, remembering something, she popped back into the house, returning with his schoolbook. 'Oh, Marcello… you forgot this yesterday,' she said, waving it above her head.

Marcello, preoccupied with balancing the cumbersome carpet, hardly turned as he called back to her. 'Oh, yes. Err, can I pick it up tomorrow?'

'Yes, yes, of course,' she said, before having a better idea. 'If you like, I could take it up to your father for you? I'll be passing there later anyway,' she lied.

'OK, that would be great. Grazie, Signora.'

'Ringraziarlo,' she exclaimed, excited as a twelve-year-old. And as she was about to step back into the house, she became caught in the vision before her. The afternoon light seeping through the dusty alleyway had crowned Marcello's head like a halo. As he trudged on with the long carpet dragging in the dirt behind him, for one moment she was transfixed; reminded of another peacemaker who'd changed his world two thousand years before.

Magical, she thought, quickly making the sign of the cross on her chest before happily skipping back inside the house, wafting Marcello's book against her face to cool herself.

As she turned to close the door, a wad of paper fell out from the folds of the book onto the doorstep. Picking it up, she unfolded the pages with interest and read the title.

'L'amore e la paura,' it said - *Love and fear*.

Fascinated by the title, she closed the door behind her and went through into the small living room, picking up her glasses from the small table on the way. She sat down in her favourite armchair by the window and began to read.

* * *

Had Marcello had cause to turn around as he staggering on up the road towards the sisters' farm, he would have seen a most extraordinary sight. From each alleyway and road junction, an ant's trail of boys started filtered out onto the high street. With oil or water-set hair and wearing their finest clothes and shoes, all resplendently furbished for the occasion, the boys started making their way up towards the Gamboccini house in droves.

From the road leading down from the Cessero Villa, Armond Cessero appeared like a prince. He was carrying the expensive vase he'd acquired from Sorrentino's earlier in the day, which was now wrapped extravagantly in golden bows and ribbons and expensive wrapping paper. Dressed in an exquisite black suit – his hair, only an hour before, having been styled by the best barber in Portoforno who had been paid handsomely to leave his salon on his busiest afternoon to attend to Armond's needs – he walked as if he were a work of art. Steering well clear of the crowd, Armond walked regally on up towards the Gamboccini house, avoiding any kind of banal banter with the rest of his peers.

On his arrival, he made his way brazenly up to the front of the queue. Ignoring the silent scorn of the boys who had been first in line, he placed his gift onto the doorstep and made one last check of his impeccable attire. Using a window's reflection, he checked his hairstyle for any last minute tweaks, blissfully unaware of the giggles from the boys behind him and Marcello's imminent arrival at the Calonne farm.

THE BOTTLE

From inside the shady hallway, Rosetta gracefully made her way along the corridor towards the front door. On opening it, a flood of sunlight poured into the dimly lit passageway and there, caught in the sunburst, was Marcello. With the Tallocci carpet slung over his shoulders, he looked thrashed by the day's events with sweat glowing from every pore of his laboured body.

'Oh, Marcello, come in, come in!' she exclaimed, standing to one side and opening the door wider for him to pass through.

Marcello staggered into the hallway and dropped the heavy carpet onto the cool mosaic floor, nearly falling over himself in the process.

'Who is It, sister?' Leonora called through from the winter garden.

'It's Marcello, sister. He's managed it too!' she added, closing the door behind him, returning the hallway to its customary dim light. Taking the fatigued boy by the arm, she stepped over the carpet and guided him through the hall and out into the winter garden beyond.

* * *

'We've been wondering where you'd got to,' Leonora said, as they entered the room.

She was sitting in exactly the same position as before, wearing identical clothes. With the tea tray laid out before her, it seemed to Marcello that all life stopped in the house whenever someone left.

'We'd given you up for dead,' she continued and the sisters chuckled together. 'Sister, I'm sure Signor Romero could do with a glass of your excellent lemonade,' she added.

Before Marcello had a chance to protest and express his eagerness to make his penultimate deal of the day and leave, Rosetta obediently got up and tottered off.

'So, Marcello, you managed it. How wonderful. It will look delightful in the hallway,' Leonora said, taking a closer look at him. She scanned his dusty attire before patting the wicker chair beside her. 'My dear boy, you look exhausted. Do come and sit down.'

'Grazie, Leonora, but...' With a pained expression, Marcello tried to convey his impatience to leave, but his silent protest fell on deaf ears. Reluctantly, he sat down.

Rosetta re-entered the room with a glass in one hand and a jug of lemonade in the other, the sound of ice splintering invitingly on top. Once again, he found his saliva glands betray him at the sound of the ice and the bitter smell of the pungent liquid. Giving in to his monumental thirst, Marcello resigned himself to a quick drink.

'Oh, what perfect timing, sister. The poor boy looks like a wilting hydrangea.' Leonora laughed, as Marcello watched Rosetta place the glass on the table and pour the cool lemonade into it. She passed the glass to Marcello.

He lifted it to his lips and felt the cool bite of the sweet liquid. Unable to resist, he downed it in one. With a smile, Rosetta leaned over and topped him up and, at that moment, the grandfather clock in the corner of the room reached its fourth chime.

Damn!

Marcello sprang to his feet, nearly knocking the jug of lemonade from Rosetta's grasp. 'Oh, scusi, Rosetta.'

Calmly, Leonora patted his chair again. 'Yes, yes, we know, Marcello. But you can hardly go rushing off in the state you're in. Now come and sit down and enjoy another glass of this lovely lemonade sister has made for you.'

Rosetta went back to topping up his glass as he reluctantly sat down again, knowing there was little he'd be able to do to get them to hurry anything.

'Ah, young love eh, sister?' Leonora continued, her eyes glazing over in reminiscence. Rosetta smiled politely and nodded as Leonora gazed dreamily out of the windows and onto the vineyards beyond. 'Sister, do you remember your first date?'

Rosetta nodded nostalgically as Marcello started looking between them in desperation.

'Mine was Roberto Giovanni,' Leonora sighed. 'He looked so grand that day. We were all in love with him, if I remember rightly. Such a handsome man. Whatever happened to him, anyway?'

'…the Great War.'

'Ah, yes, the Great War,' she repeated, sadly. 'What a tragedy.'

Marcello finished his last swig of his lemonade and started twitching his knee up and down. Seemingly unaware, Leonora looked across at her sister with a frown. 'Who was your first date, sister? I've quite forgotten,' and without waiting for an answer, her eyes lit up. '…the Romaldi boy, of course. Now, there was a handsome chap. I remember him well.'

Marcello, had heard enough. He sprang to his feet. 'Scusi, sisters but...' he started, but Leonora was one step ahead of him.

'Ah, yes. But of course, Marcello,' she said, cutting him off. 'Sister, would you be so kind as to bring a bottle of the liqueur up from the cellars for Signor Romero. I fear he'll explode if we don't let him go.'

Rosetta nodded, silently rose from her wicker chair and wandered over to an antique mahogany dresser sitting to the side of the room. The surface was blanketed with plant-pots and cuttings which she moved to one side before ceremoniously picking up an unusually shaped bottle from the shelf.

'Oh, you already have a bottle. How clever of you,' Leonora smiled, obviously impressed at her sister's forethought. Loving stroking the dust off it, Rosetta brought it back to the table and passed it over to Leonora to give to Marcello. 'And richly deserved too, if I may say so, my dear,' Leonora said, pressing the beautifully hand-scribed labelled bottle into Marcello's eager hands.

Marcello immediately started shuffling his way backwards across the room, bowing incessantly. 'Mille grazie. Mille, mille grazie, sisters.'

'To you too, my dear… to you too,' Leonora said, waving her hand regally at him. She looked across at her sister and added, 'Would you see the little Romeo to the door, dear?' Rosetta nodded again and started escorting Marcello back down the grand hallway towards the front door.

* * *

Hearing the front door close in the background a few moments later, Leonora reclined her head into the wicker chair and sighed deeply. Letting a warm satisfied feeling wash over her, she listened to the peacefully familiar sound of Rosetta's heels tapping on the marble floor. And, as her sister busied herself unrolling the Turkish carpet that, thanks to Marcello Romero, had at long last made it's way back home to rest in its rightful place in their hallway, she allowed herself to be immersed once again in nostalgic thoughts.

* * *

Marcello came tearing out of the farm gates with the bottle of liqueur gripped tightly in his right hand. At full sprint, he headed off down the street towards the village. As he approached the Bellini house, he saw the tail-end of the queue of boys trailing back from the Gamboccini home. Slipping through the garden gates, he rapped impatiently on the butcher's back door. Receiving no immediate answer, he started knocking more frantically, looking in through the window and pressing his nose up to the glass.

Suddenly the door flew open. And there, bursting with the power of Zeus, stood the mighty Bellini in his customary string vest. 'What is it *now,* Romero?' he thundered.

Marcello simply held the bottle of liqueur out to him and watched his expression change.

Bellini's eyes grew in astonishment, almost popping out of his oversized head. 'Wha..? How the hell did you pull that off, Romero?'

Marcello smiled inwardly. 'I...' he started, but Bellini waved his hand at him impatiently.

'Never mind, it doesn't interest me.'

Without waiting, he burst out of the house and started across the garden, shaking his head from side to side in wonder. 'How did he do that?' he mumbled to himself as he pounded over the dry dirt towards the chicken coop with Marcello close on his heels. On the other side of the garden, they reached a ramshackle wooden hut, the walls made of pieces of wood nailed haphazardly together. Bellini pulled the flimsy door open and thrust his burly hand into the cage.

Seconds later, the hand reappeared holding a cockerel around the neck, the animal flapping wildly in protest. In one movement, Bellini thrust the crazed animal towards Marcello and lunged for the bottle of liqueur with his other hand. Marcello had no option but to take the squirming creature from him. He squinted and held it at arms length for fear of its rapid wing movement taking one of his eyes out. Bellini then set off back across the garden, leaving Marcello to fight with the creature.

'Scusi, Signor Bellini, do you have, something I can put the cockerel in?'

'Yeah, sure, Romero, but it'll cost you another bottle!' Bellini roared, belly laughing at his own joke as he returned to his back door. He held the bottle of liqueur up in the air like a trophy and waved it at Marcello. 'I hope that damn thing gives you as much pleasure as this will me,' he added, stepping inside the house and slamming the door behind him.

Unsure of what to do next, Marcello stood helplessly in the middle of the garden trying to retain hold of the cockerel which was filling the air with its feathers. Thinking quickly, he set off out of the garden and across the road, being careful not to alert the attention of the ever diminishing line of boys outside the Gamboccini house. With the cockerel kicking and flapping in his arms, Marcello reached the harbour wall and scanned the area for inspiration.

Yes!

His gaze fell upon an old lobster pot lying on a pile of threadbare nets. He sprang swiftly over the wall and landed precariously onto the oily stones. Grabbing the pot, he popped the protesting cockerel in. Then, picking up a piece of fishing net from the pile underneath, he tied up the gaping hole in the side; enough to hold it together for the short journey back to the Gamboccini's. Satisfied with his handiwork, he picked up the caged cockerel and jumped back over the harbour wall and, with what must have been the last burst of power his exhausted muscles could muster, he tore off up the road towards the Gamboccini house to meet with his destiny.

THE PRESENTATION

To Marcello's relief as he ran up to the Gamboccini house, he saw a row of five boys still waiting patiently outside. He took his place at the back of the line, at last catching his breath and allowing his heart to slow. Suddenly, one by one, the boys in front of him started nudging each other and turning back to look at him. Their mouths dropped open. Pointing at him, they fell into hysterics. Some of the boys, who were waiting inside the house, poked their heads up at the window, trying to see what was causing all the commotion. On getting an eyeful of Marcello, they joined the growing gaggle of sniggers.

What is your problem? Marcello thought, before catching a glimpse of himself in a window's reflection. Hair in disarray; clothes dusty and crumpled with patches of sweat under the arms and, saddled with the butcher's mangy bird in a stinking old lobster pot, he suddenly understood why their amusement was so intense. He looked a terrible state. In an attempt to improve his appearance, he licked his free hand and started pressing it through his hair, the pathetic gesture only serving to ignite another bout of frenzied hysteria amongst the delighted audience.

Marcello suddenly heard a familiar voice calling to him from around the corner of the house. 'Cello… *Cello!*' He turned to see his father waving impatiently at him.

Great timing! Marcello ignored him and went back to dealing with his appearance.

'Marcello! Come *here!*'

Realising his father was not to be deterred, Marcello stepped around the corner just as one more boy was ushered inside the house, shortening the queue down to three.

'Papa, this is not a good time,' he snapped.

Silently, Francesco opened the bag he had in his right hand and pulled out a freshly ironed shirt and trousers.

'Papa...' Marcello whimpered, his heart melting at his father's thoughtfulness. Without another word, Francesco took the cage from his son so he could change into his clean clothes. As he dressed, Marcello was astounded to see that his father had chosen the exact clothes he had left in a crumple mess on his bedroom floor that morning, albeit now in much better condition.

Taking his dirty clothes from him, Francesco tucked the items back into the bag and, when his son had finished doing up the last button, he pulled out a comb from his back pocket and passed it to him. 'You go and show these boys what a man is,' he said.

For the first time in years, Marcello saw the warm and deep emotions which had been so painfully lost since the departure of his mother, shimmer once again in his father's eyes. 'Papa...' Marcello started, not really sure what he wanted to say; apologise for last night's anger; thank him for his thoughtfulness, or just hug him for finally accepting his feelings for Elena.

'You're a good boy, Cello,' he said, giving his son's hair a fond ruffle. Suddenly realising what he'd done, he tried to push it back in place again. 'Oh, scusi, Cello.'

Marcello smiled, ran the comb quickly through his hair again and then passed it back to his father in exchange for the makeshift cage.

'Auguri, Cello, tanti auguri,' Francesco said.

Grateful for the good wishes, Marcello took one last look at his father and then dashed back around the corner to take up his place in the queue, just as the boy before him stepped into the Gamboccini house.

* * *

Down in the village, Riccardo and Paulo were still sitting on the harbour wall together, gazing at Tito. Inspired by the monotony of Tito's rhythmic throws, they were swinging their legs backwards and forwards in time to the thuds. Riccardo was just in the midst of contemplating whether or not to go up to the Gamboccini house to find out how Marcello had got on, when, from around the corner of the high street, three beautiful girls appeared, arm in arm like a heavenly apparition. Forgetting the previous day's beating, he slid off the wall, wincing as his bottom scraped the stonework. Beside him, Paulo did the same.

Transfixed by their sultry confidence, Riccardo watched as the girls sauntered slowly on down towards them.

Tito was the last to react. He turned just as they wondered by, his ball slipping from his grasp and rolling out into the middle of the road.

Riccardo instantly recognised the three of them as school friends of Elena. But now, free of their staid blue and white school uniforms, they looked earth-shattering. They strolled down between the three of them with their heads held high. Suddenly, with a seductive swing of the head, the stunning redhead turned to face Paulo.

'Not joining all the rest of the boys at Elena's house then, Paulo?' she said, raising an eyebrow, '…I'm impressed.'

'Err, no, um, Marcello, Elena, err...' Paulo stuttered, evidently dumb-struck by her beauty.

Riccardo gave him a sharp nudge in the ribs with his elbow, kick-starting him again.

'Err, no,' he mumbled.

For Riccardo, time slowed down as the racy brunette turned to him, her hair flipping to one side as she did so.

'Heard you might need some liniment rubbing into those sores of yours, Riccardo?' And, with a slight dip of the head, she nodded towards to his backside with a cheeky smile. Stunned, Riccardo nodded and ran his hand over the seat of his shorts without once breaking her gaze.

Spotting Tito's ball, which was lying in the street in front of them, the last of the three girls brought the others to a standstill. Bending her knees in a ladylike manner, her fashionable skirt raising up her shapely legs, she stooped down and picked it up. Turning to him, she gave him a scandalous wink and effortlessly flung the ball at him at full force. It hit him in the solar plexus at a tremendous speed, almost winding him. Without saying a word, she dusted off her hands, lifted her eyebrow and linked arms again with her friends before leading them off down towards the village square.

Captivated, Riccardo, Paulo and Tito's eyes followed them as they went.

Tito was the first to break the silence. 'Did you feel the power of that?' he mumbled, rubbing his stomach where the ball had hit him.

Without taking his eyes off the girls, Riccardo slowly nodded in agreement. Then, breaking him out of his trance, the brunette turned, threw him a wanton smile and turned back, her silky hair once again whisking up into the bright sunlight like a model's from a magazine shampoo advert.

'What the hell are we doing?' he burst, at last coming to his senses. '*Come on*!' He slapped Paulo in the chest and, with his friends in hot pursuit, set off down the road after them.

* * *

The entrance hall to the Gamboccini home was as grand as the Calonne sisters', albeit with much more life. A beautiful Turkish carpet was spread across the bright marbled floor. Against one wall was an old wooden entrance table with a grandfather clock standing next to it, its peaceful ticking adding an air of serenity to the room. In the centre of the large hallway, leading majestically up to a wooden upstairs-landing, was an imposing wooden staircase. Along its tiers were old family portraits depicting the family trait of pride and formality.

When summoned, Marcello entered the front door. Taking in the resplendence of the room for the first time, his eyes drifted from the décor, to the ensemble of boys around him. At the bottom of the staircase was a table full of ornate and expensive gifts. Strewn across the floor beside it was a pile of wrapping paper and Marcello's heart took a leap as his eyes moved from that, to the short fat figure standing dominantly on the bottom step of the stairway.

Signor Gamboccini was busy placing the last present on the table next to Armond's magnificent vase. As he finished, he lifted his eyes to look at Marcello. A deathly expectant hush filled the room.

In the silence, Signor Gamboccini's mouth dropped open.

Marcello could hear the delighted onlookers biting back their splutters as Signor Gamboccini gaped at his appearance. Although smarter, dressed in the freshly laundered clothes Francesco had brought for him, he was still sweating profusely from his forehead. His shoes and socks were caked in dust, and a few cuts and bruises were visible on his hands and arms. But what made the man's face start to burn with rage was when his gaze drifted from Marcello's face, to the gift that was dangling from Marcello's right hand.

Marcello suddenly realised how it must look to everyone but him; a beaten-up lobster pot held together with twine and stinking of fish with a mangy cockerel flapping about in the cage in a bid to escape its makeshift confines.

'*What the*..!' Signor Gamboccini exploded and the other boys in the room, unable to contain their amusement any longer, fell into hysterics.

Signor Gamboccini started waving his hands about in rage, trying to find the words to match his obvious indignation. His wife, standing beside him, caught his eye as he looked across in astonishment, searching for some sort of explanation as to the boy's actions. Marcello saw her cast him a pleading look and put her hands together in a begging motion, but evidently he was having none of it.

'*You come into my home... on this day,*' he steamed, winding himself up into a rage, '*...and you bring that!*' He pointed at the ramshackle cage in Marcello's hand. 'Is this your idea of a joke? You bring *that* as a gift of respect?'

In the doorway, Signor Gamboccini's wife bit down on the knuckles of her right hand as Marcello opened his mouth to speak. He didn't get chance to react. 'You shame both yourself and your family. And you bring disrespect into my house!' Signor Gamboccini continued.

At that moment, there was a creak from upstairs and everyone in the room except for Marcello and Signor Gamboccini, looked up to its source.

Elena Gamboccini stepped out of an upstairs doorway.

The atmosphere in the room changed instantly. All the boys gasped and stared up in reverend silence as she gently closed the door behind her and walked across to the top of the stairs.

Marcello, feeling the silence descend upon the room, looked up. Ignoring Signor Gamboccini's livid stare, he too lost himself in the moment, watching in awe as she coasted down the grand staircase. She looked stunning, wearing a simple knee-length patterned summer dress which cascaded around her torso like the wings of a thousand angels. She eased down the grand stairway, her waist-long shadow-black hair flowing like Thai silk behind her.

As she reached the bottom of the stairs, Elena edged up behind her father and leaned down to whisper in his ear. Marcello's heart raced as both Elena and her father's eyes settled upon him. As she continued to whisper in her father's ear, Marcello lifted his head slightly, taking in the smell of her light perfume which had started to permeate the air of the hallway.

And then he noticed it.

As she continued whispering, Signor Gamboccini's expression started to change. First, the frown on his forehead eased. Then, his head tipped to one side. And, after a few more seconds, his eyes started to open, wider and wider. At last, a smile appeared on his chubby face.

Clearly satisfied, Elena pulled back. She let her arms drop to her side and watched, as her father, like a coiled spring, let out a gasp.

Suddenly, with his arms outstretched, he stepped forward towards Marcello. Marcello flinched, afraid for his life, until the elated man wrapped him in his burly grasp. 'My boy. My dear, dear boy!' he wailed, hugging him with delight.

The boys around him gasped with devastation, obviously unable to understand what had just happened. Whilst Marcello was being bear-hugged by the little man, one by one, they rose to their feet and, with a slouch in their step, started to trail out of the house.

Over her father's shoulder, Marcello caught Elena's smile. Although his eyes were almost being squeezed out of his head, he managed to smile back. His eyes then drifted over to Signora Gamboccini who, much to his surprise, was watching the whole affair with relief. What happened to the woman he'd bumped into yesterday? Marcello wondered as she shrugged and smiled with delight at her daughter.

Eventually, Signor Gamboccini let Marcello go. Leaning over, he took the cage from Marcello's grasp and, with one last grateful pinch of Marcello's cheek, turned and left the room.

From of the corner of the room, Marcello detected a movement in the shadows. Standing in the wings and out of sight of everyone, was Armond Cessero. He was waving his finger at Marcello in warning, reminding him, in no uncertain terms, of their deal. It was a bitter pill to swallow at such a wonderful moment but, acknowledging his promise, Marcello nodded. He then turned back quickly as he felt Elena step down off the stairs and take his hand.

* * *

Leaning over the table to pick up her light blue cardigan, Elena kissed her mother on the cheek and, with a victorious smile, led Marcello out of the front door and into the beautiful evening sunlight, to taste her first night of freedom… and her first date.

THE CAFÉ

The sun sat low in the sky and a backdrop of pastel red clouds framed Marcello and Elena as they walked down the high street together, hand in hand. Marcello's heart was full of emotions he'd never experienced in one moment before; expectation, joy, elation and a warm feeling of achievement. It was futile to try to hold back the huge grin that was frozen on his face as he strolled down towards Gianni's café with the most beautiful girl in the village on his arm.

* * *

To Elena's surprise, the roads were packed on both sides with villagers; villagers, who were obviously inquisitive as to the outcome of her father's decision. But why, she couldn't comprehend. They had gathered to line the streets and, as the two of them passed, some were waving items above heads at him. She could only look at him in wonder, his face glowing with pride.

A few of the boys that had been at her house earlier were now leaning up against the wall with their arms crossed in front of them. As they passed, however, they didn't sneer – as so often happened when boys had been rejected by other fathers – instead, she saw them nodding with respect. *Strange.*

Further on down the road, the Calonne sisters were flapping their hands together and cuddling each other with glee, evidently ecstatic for them both. *But why?*

On the other side of the road she recognised Signora Tallocci, cuddling her own shoulders with a far-away expression in her eyes and a big smile on her face.

She looked over at Marcello, hoping he'd be able to tell her what this unusual reception was all about. In her sixteen years of being an onlooker, it was truly a first. But he just grinned at her, which only made her already broad smile surge into a wave of giggles. Relaxing into the moment and, with a permanent smile set on her lips, she allowed herself to enjoy the moment and the extraordinary attention they were receiving.

* * *

From a side road, Francesco appeared. Standing amongst the other villagers, he watched with pride as Marcello and Elena wandered by. He had to admit, it was astounding to see just what his son had achieved for their small village in the last twenty four hours, although quite what he had done and how he had done it was beyond him. *That* he had done it, though, was astonishing. And, by looking at the crowd, he wasn't alone in that thought.

Suddenly, Marcello's eyes found him amongst the crowd and with a tear in his eye and happiness in his heart, Francesco conveyed his feelings of pride for his son with a simple nod.

* * *

As he nodded to his father in the crowd, Marcello felt Elena grip his hand tighter. He turned to look into her smiling face and, at that moment, felt like he'd found heaven. *It doesn't get much better than this*, he thought to himself, until a few moments later when he spotted Riccardo, Tito and Paulo on the far side of the road with three stunning girls draped on their arms. He almost did a double take.

Riccardo, obviously enjoying his best friend's confusion, just tipped his head to one side and nodded with a discerning grin as if to say; *you're not the only one who got lucky today, my friend.* Marcello smiled, happy that the boys, who'd given him so much over the last twenty four hours, had received something in return.

* * *

Back up the high street, the crowd had dispersed as the villagers made their way off home. Signora Tallocci was still lost in her thoughts; reminded of her first date many moons before with a dashing young man who, she now realised, she still held a torch for.

Spotting the Calonne sisters making their way back up the high street towards their farm, she snapped out of her nostalgia and, still gripping Marcello's schoolbook firmly in her hands, ran over to them.

'Scusi, sisters,' she called, picking up her pace.

The sisters turned.

'Ah, Signora Tallocci, how nice to see you,' Leonora said.

She came along side them. 'Hello,' she said nervously. 'I'd... I'd like to apologise for my behaviour.'

'Oh, that's not necessary, dear.'

'No, I think it is,' she insisted. 'I have been very unfair. After the death of my husband, I… I don't know… I was so upset, I suppose. And the things I said were totally unfounded.'

'Dear, we both know what it's like to lose someone,' Leonora assured her, and Rosetta nodded in agreement. 'Sometimes you look for someone to blame. Something to try and take the pain away. Really, we do understand. No harm done.' Suddenly, her face lit up. 'How about a nice cup of tea? We're just on our way home. Would you like to join us? It's been such an exciting day.'

'Thank you, really, I'd love to,' Signora Tallocci said, holding up Marcello's schoolbook. 'But I have something I must do this afternoon, I'm afraid. Maybe tomorrow?'

'Fine dear; whenever you have the time. We're always happy to have visitors... aren't we, sister?' Rosetta nodded heartily again and, as they turned to leave, Mrs Tallocci watched as Leonora sidled up to her sister with excitement. 'Oh, what a lovely day, sister.'

Watching them go, Signora Tallocci let a deep and satisfying sigh escape her lips. After a moment or two's reflection, she turned and, her fingers tingling with excitement, scuttled off in the direction of the Romero house.

* * *

Marcello and Elena arrived at Gianni's small harbour cafe that held the most incomparable views across the whole bay. Under orders from Gianni himself, a place was reserved for them both on the veranda outside. The waiter, dressed in a beautifully starched white open-necked shirt with a white apron covering his charcoal trousers, pulled back two chairs at a table as they approached.

Marcello sat down and the waiter, sliding the chair gracefully under Elena as she sat, whipped his tea cloth across the table, removing an imaginary crumb from the spotless table cloth. He picked up the reserved sign and, flipping the tea cloth over his arm, disappeared back inside the cafe.

For the first time that day, they sat together in silence; a silence that Marcello found surprisingly comfortable. Slowly, as the breath of the warm sea air gently caressed his face and they took in the spectacular view as if for the first time, it dawned on Marcello that he knew almost nothing about this wonderful girl. Instinctively, anticipating a break in the silence, Marcello turned to Elena.

'That was quite a turn out. What did we do to deserve that?' she asked, returning his smile.

Marcello, reluctant to explain the whole story on such a magical occasion, feigned an unknowing shrug.

'So, tell me,' she continued, changing the subject, 'what do you write in that book of yours?'

'Sorry?' Marcello stuttered, suddenly taken aback. It hadn't even occurred to him that she had paid him so much attention as he sat outside her window, day after day, for as long as he could remember. He felt his face flush.

'…your book. You sit outside our house each day, scribbling in that book of yours. What do you write about?'

'Oh, that!' he replied, feeling like a boy caught with his hands in the cookie jar. 'Nothing really, just stuff. Thoughts. Ideas.'

'What sort of ideas?'

Checking for a sign of genuine interest, Marcello looked into her eyes before answering.

She held his gaze.

'Oh, I don't know really. Things just pop into my head. Rhymes, sort of. Poetry. My friends think I'm a bit of a dreamer.' He let out a strained laugh, hoping his embarrassment wasn't too obvious.

'Really? That's the boys we just passed isn't it? They seem really nice.'

'Yeah, they're great. Really.'

'I bet they only tease you. Mine do the same,' she assured him.

'Really? Oh, I haven't seen you with any... err... Not that I... err...' *Aw, get it together, Marcello!*

'That's OK, I know what you mean,' she smiled, making him feel much more at ease and at that moment the waiter stepped out of the cafe carrying two glasses of water and the menus.

He placed the glasses gracefully on the table and offered a menu to Elena. 'Signora.'

Elena looked up at him and smiled, holding her hand up to refuse the menu. 'Grazie Signor, just an espresso for me please.' She smiled politely and then looked across at Marcello, who nodded in agreement.

'Yes, for me too. Grazie.'

Thankful for not having to foot an expensive bill, he wondered if Elena was only too well aware of that fact and had acted accordingly. A girl of such a solid upbringing, it would hardly surprise him. But that only made him wonder if that was the only reason she was being so nice to him.

The waiter slipped the menus swiftly under his arm and nodded in agreement. 'Of course,' he said before walking swiftly back into the cafe.

Elena continued. 'I'm sorry if my father seems a little strict. Most of the friends I have are from school and I suppose he's worried about his only daughter falling in with *bad company.*' She made quotation marks with her fingers, emphasising the last two words and smiled at him again.

Wow, that smile!

They both laughed. 'Oh, that's OK,' Marcello said, allowing himself to relax, 'I guess I'd be the same if I had a daughter as beautiful... err...'

Idiot!

He could have kicked himself. He quickly grabbed his glass of water and took a sip.

Elena simply reached across the table and placed her hand over his. 'Thank you,' she said, giving it a light squeeze and at that moment the waiter re-appeared carrying two small cups of espresso.

Marcello, half glad of the intrusion and half wanting the moment to last for ever, sat up as the waiter placed the cups down onto the table with experienced precision.

'Signora… Signor.'

He bowed, repositioned the tea cloth on his arm and strode professionally back inside the cafe, leaving Marcello and Elena to enjoy the silence and sip their coffee in the glow of the rich evening sunlight.

From the right hand side of the cafe, Marcello's attention was suddenly caught by a sharp movement. Standing by the side of the delicatessen was Armond. He was waving his arms about, evidently bored of waiting for Marcello to disappear so he could take up his rightful place beside Elena.

Reminded of their deal, Marcello felt a hole open up in the pit of his stomach. Playing for time, he leaned over and picked up his coffee cup. His mind was racing. With all he'd had to organise in the last twenty four hours, it hadn't even occurred to him to make a contingency plan for this part of the deal.

Fool!

He sipped at his espresso again. Knowing there was no way out, he nodded, just enough for Armond to see he had acknowledged his presence.

What do you do now?

Elena must have sensed a shift in the atmosphere. She looked over at him with concern. 'Is everything OK?'

'Oh yeah, fine, fine,' Marcello lied, chewing himself up inside at the thought of leaving this wonderful girl to the jaws of Armond Cessero.

'Only you seem...' she pressed.

'No, really… Err, I must...' Reluctantly, he shrugged and pointed back towards the toilets inside the café.

'Oh, OK,' she said.

He took one last look at her angelic face, placed his cup back onto the tiny saucer and got up.

Walking back into the café, he felt bitter at the resounding full stop he was putting on the end of their precious first date; dates that, over the decades, had seen the lives of hundreds of villagers before them changed forever.

* * *

Armond, from his vantage point outside the delicatessen, looked on as Marcello mumbled something indistinct to Elena, rose out of his seat and walked back into the cafe. Taking his cue, he made a quick check of his appearance in a window's reflection.

Perfect.

Licking his hand, he brushed it through his hair one last time, he loosened the collar of his silk shirt and, with a confident shrug of the shoulders, set off towards the cafe where his prey was now sitting alone.

* * *

Stuck in the toilets, Marcello was pacing backwards and forwards in the small tiled area like a caged animal. The tip of his middle finger was in his mouth as he chewed frantically on his fingernail. *What are you going to do now, then?* He was livid with himself. No contingency plan. No backup resources left at his disposal - although just what that could have been, he had no idea. The thing was, he had ignored all the training his father had ever taught him about survival. *'The seven P's; Proper-Pre-Planning-Prevents-Pathetically-Poor-Performance.'*

Lot of good remembering that now!

Suddenly, his eyes noticed the small window just above the basin. He dashed over and picked up the makeshift wastepaper bin beside the sink. As he up-turned the rusty ten-litre tomato tin, a few dried tissues fell out onto the floor. Ignoring the mess, he clambered up onto its base and reached up to the window. He lifted the catch and tried to push the window out with the ball of his hand.

Nothing.

Glued shut with old paint! He started to hammer against the frame in an attempt to force it open. After a few tries, it broke loose. Pushing it out as far as it would go, he started to force his slight body out through the gap. But as he lifted his foot onto the sink for more leverage, the metal bin slipped out from underneath him and flew across the tiled floor, crashing into the wall opposite. The sound from inside the cafe must have been thunderous.

Ignoring it, Marcello managed to get the first half of his small frame out through the tiny hole and onto the raised ground outside the window. Squeezing the rest of his body out, he pulled himself to his feet at the rear of the café and started dusting himself off.

...And now?

He couldn't help himself. Taking flight, he quickly ran around to the side of the building and positioned himself outside the delicatessen where Armond had been waiting only moments earlier. Chancing a peek, he popped his head around the corner. He was just in time to see Armond slip a petrol-lighter out of his breast pocket and light the tip of a cigarette. Marcello could only watch on helplessly as Armond, in one practiced motion, casually slid down into his chair and let his arm glide behind the back of Elena's seat.

Marcello's mouth ran dry. *What are you doing here, Marcello? Don't watch.* But he was spellbound.

Relaxed, Armond placed the lighter back in the breast pocket of his shirt, coolly allowing a cloud of cigarette smoke to cascade out from the corner of his mouth.

He turned towards her.

Devastated, Marcello continued to stare at them. He felt sick with desperation but was unable to drag his eyes away from the sight of his first date disintegrating into nothingness before his very eyes. Seconds later, Armond hammered the final nail into the coffin. As the waiter finished delivering a bottle of Champagne to the table, Armond put out his cigarette and, as smoothly as a shark through water, slid his free hand across onto Elena's knee.

Unable to watch any more, Marcello whipped his head back around the corner of the building. His heart was beating like an antelope in chase as he bit back the urge to throw up. He stood there for a minute, unable to stop his mind racing.

Is there nothing more you can do? But nothing would come to him.

What seemed like an age later, he checked his legs would still carry him, pushed himself away from the comforting support of the wall and strode off and away from the cafe, leaving Armond to reap the spoils of battle with his first and only love.

THE ESSAY

Signora Tallocci arrived outside Marcello's house, still gripping onto his schoolbook for comfort. With her heart beating like a teenager, she tapped lightly on the front door. A few moments later, as she nervously flicked her fingers across her fringe for the umpteenth time, the squeak of the door handle sounded and there, in the doorway, stood her childhood sweetheart.

'Maria, hello,' Francesco said, wiping his hands on his trousers, visibly flustered by her presence.

Signora Tallocci fingered Marcello's schoolbook again. 'Hello, Francesco. I hope I'm not disturbing you?'

'No, no. Please come in,' he said, as they exchanged an uncomfortable handshake. He gestured for her to enter the small living room.

'Err, I only came to bring back Marcello's school book,' she said.

Village gossip had had her believe the reclusive lifestyle he'd led after his wife's sudden departure three years before and she had felt awkward making the visit. Throwing caution to the wind anyway, she'd taken the chance Marcello had given her.

'He left it at my house yesterday,' she continued. 'And, what with all his running around, I offered to bring it back for him.'

'That's very kind of you. I'm sure he'll appreciate it. Thank you. Do come in.'

She stepped into the house, marvelling at its freshness as she entered the living room. The curtains were open, revealing beautifully clean windows and a fresh bowl of sunflowers sat in the middle of the uncluttered table. Hardly the sight she had expected from a supposed love-sick recluse. Impressed with its cleanliness, she almost forgot for a moment her excuse for coming.

'Actually there was something else,' she said, eager to keep the conversation flowing.

He leaned over to close the door behind her and in that split second, their eyes met.

Lost in the intensity of his mahogany eyes clad by the suntanned wrinkles, she smiled back, transfixed. It had been a long time since they had been that close, but at that moment it suddenly seemed like only yesterday.

Breaking the moment, he gestured to his armchair beside the fire place and, as she walked over and perched herself on the edge of the seat, Francesco sat himself down on the stool opposite.

'Oh, scusi, scusi,' he said, springing to his feet again. 'I'm not used to having guests. Can I get you something to drink?'

'No. Thank you, Francesco.'

As he retook his seat, she nervously pressed the creases out of her dress and took a deep breath.

'The reason I've come is I have a little confession to make. As you know, I have done little writing since my husband died. I mostly read these days. From time to time, I come across works that inspire and move me. But none, more so than this…' With that, she pulled out of her pocket the wad of paper Marcello had left at her house, entitled *L'amore e la paura*. She passed it to Francesco. 'This fell from Marcello's schoolbook yesterday,' she continued. 'And, although I feel a little ashamed to have read it, I must tell you, it's an extraordinary piece of writing. If this really is Marcello's work... and, judging by the subject matter, I believe it is… then your son truly has a God-given talent.'

* * *

Francesco started to flick hastily through the pages. 'I know someone who will be *very* happy to see this,' he said, at last, realising that Marcello had been one step ahead of them all the whole time. 'Thank you, Maria.'

He looked back up into her beautiful cornflower blue eyes; eyes that had so stunned him on their first date together all those years ago.

Why did you let her go?

So much had happened in the last twenty four hours to shake him up; his argument with Marcello; the realisation of his years of selfishness; Marcello's achievements; the essay; and now Maria Tallocci – his first date –

sitting directly opposite him in his own living room, those liquid blue eyes of hers as entrancing as they were all those years ago.

He suddenly realised he hadn't spoken for a long moment. 'This calls for a celebration,' he said, rising from his seat and making his way across the room. 'Are you sure you won't join me?'

'Well, in that case, I'd love to,' she said, giving in to his enthusiasm. 'It will be the first drink I've had in a long time,' she added, as Francesco returned with a bottle of Asti Cinzano.

'And for me, the last,' he said, pouring the two glasses.

He held up his glass, '…to Marcello.'

'To Marcello,' she agreed, meeting his glass in the toast and then taking a sip. Her face instantly turned from shock to amusement at the unexpected hit of the bubbles and they laughed together.

* * *

He sat down opposite her. After taking a moment to enjoy the chilled bubbles' dance across her tongue, she opened her mouth to break the silence. He beat her to it.

'So, tell me, how have you been? It's been a while since I've seen you around the village.'

'Yes. I'm fine now, really.' She settled herself back into his armchair, her hand subconsciously caressing the arm-rest. 'It takes a while for the pain to go, you know.'

Francesco nodded. She looked at him, unsure of whether to ask the question. 'And you?'

'Oh, you know. Bitterness is a dangerous emotion,' he laughed self-consciously. 'It eats you from the inside out. Before you know it, you're looking in the mirror at an empty shell.'

They smiled, letting the wisdom of his words hang in the air.

Suddenly, Francesco leaned forward and placed his glass down onto the table in front of them. 'Anyway, Maria Tallocci,' he announced with bravado. 'How about we let the past take care of itself and I make you a bowl of pasta... fisherman's style?' He stood. '…if you have nothing else planned for this evening, that is?'

She looked up at him with a radiant smile. Unsure of whether the emotions tearing round her body were to do with the alcohol, or for all those years as a teenager wanting to hear an invitation like that coming from those lips.

'Signor Romero, I would be honoured,' she said, entering into the spirit. She stood and, as he made his way across the room towards the kitchen, she followed with a spring in her step.

* * *

At the Cessero mansion, there was an eerie calm in the air. With the sound of his house keys scratching about in the lock and the thump of the front door being knocked back against the wall, Armond shattered it.

The sound of someone staggering into the grand hallway and falling like a lumpen sack onto the cool marble floor, stirred his father in his study. He'd waited for hours for his son's return and jumped out of his expensive leather reading-chair at the sounds that were emanating from down the corridor.

'Armond, is that you?' he called, angrily.

Hearing no answer, he placed his newspaper onto the small Chesterfield table and stepped out into the hallway. The sight before him made his jaw drop.

'Right, my boy, I want to see you in my study, immediately.' He watched as his son staggered to his feet. 'Have you been drinking?'

'What's it to you?' Armond slurred.

Signor Cessero was beside himself. 'What's it to me? *What's it to me?* I'm your father, that's what!'

'…could have fooled me.'

With a chuckle, Armond stumbled against the round antique table that was standing between them, precariously rocking the expensive bone-china vase in the middle, bursting with an array of beautiful flowers.

'What did you say?' Signor Cessero's face reddened. He pointed back into his study. 'I've just about had enough of your insolence, my boy. I think you'd better get in there, before I...'

'…before you what?' Armond anticipated. 'Lay me across your knee? I didn't know you cared.'

* * *

Signora Cessero, having listened to their exchange from behind the living room door, suddenly appeared in the hallway.

'Dear, maybe this isn't a good time...'

'You keep out of it!' he barked and she smarted with shock. '*Your* son has stolen valuables from his own home and I will not accept that kind of behaviour in this house!'

'Ah, I thought hitting you in the wallet might shake some feeling out of you.' Armond said with another drunken giggle.

'I don't believe I'm hearing this! I think it's time I showed you a little discipline, my boy. Have you any idea what my father would have done to me if I...'

'Now, the two of you, that's enough!' Signora Cessero yelled

'*I said, keep out of it!*' Armond's father roared, pointing at her again.

After years of being treated like a second-class citizen in her own home, Signora Cessero thrust herself between the two of them and came face to face with her husband. '*No sir, I will not keep out of it!*'

Both Armond and his father jumped in shock.

She turned to Armond. 'You… go to your room… *immediately!*'

Armond, even drunk, was evidently sensible enough to realise this was not the time pit his will against his mother's newly found resolve and did as he was told. As he ascended the stairs, Signora Cessero turned back to her husband.

'I've had enough of this! The atmosphere of disrespect in this house is unbearable. *And yes*, I know exactly what your father would have done in this situation... exactly what *you* were about to do. And you can see where *THAT - GOT - YOU,*' she bellowed, prodding her fingers against his rib cage in time to the last three words of her sentence.

'I beg your pardon?' Signor Cessero muttered, seemingly horrified by her sudden change in character.

'I imagine you do. That boy doesn't need a disciplinarian, he needs a father,' she said, pointing at her son, who was still staggering up the staircase like a dog with its tail between its legs.

'And what do you think I work hard for every day? Giving the boy a chance in life, something *I* had to work for,' he declared, defensively.

'Why is it that every man believes that money is the only stability a father has to provide?' Having got his attention, she took a deep breath and continued with a little more decorum. 'The only thing that is going to save *our* son from growing up to be the spoilt little brat that he is, is time. He desperately wants and needs your attention. Why do you think he's doing all these things? He's screaming at you, for God's sake.'

Having decided she had made her point, she turned and walked to the bottom of the staircase. As she reached it, she turned and looked back at him. 'And, if you want any kind of respect from your son in future, I might suggest giving him a little more of your precious time.'

She turned again and started to ascend the staircase, leaving the ice-cream magnate standing in shock and, for the first time in his life, utterly speechless.

MARCELLO'S DATE

The sun had dropped below the horizon. The only natural light still peppering the village monuments was emanating from the moon reflecting off the surface of the calm ocean.

Marcello had been wandering around the village for what seemed like hours, his thoughts picking at his conscience like a pack of rabid dogs at a carcass.

Maybe Dad was right. Why did you think you could pull it off, anyway... especially with that girl? Of course she's going to fall for him... all the others do. What the hell did you expect? Her to come running out after you? Who the hell do you think you are?

He continued to torment himself as he wandered around the quiet streets, scuffing his feet in the dirt and feeling more alone than he had ever felt in his entire life. It had been hours since the catastrophe at Gianni's cafe and, with nowhere else to go, and no friends to visit even if he wanted to, he found himself back at the Gamboccini house.

He sat himself down on the familiar patch of wall, this time with his legs hanging over the opposite side and with his head turned in the direction of the shimmering black ocean. The colour, he noted, reflecting perfectly his emotional turmoil.

* * *

Behind him, in the upstairs window of the Gamboccini house, Elena walked over to her open bedroom window. She stopped dead in her tracks as she saw that confounded Romero boy sitting outside her window.

The cheek of it!

For a moment, she stood there fuming, unsure of exactly what to do. Her anger getting the better of her, she leaned across, grabbed the latch handles and slammed the windows firmly shut.

* * *

Busy wallowing in self pity, Marcello failed to notice the sound of Elena's window slamming shut. Nor, moments later, did he notice the rattle of the Gamboccini front door and the sound of rapidly approaching footsteps behind him.

'Who the hell do you think you are?'

He turned in shock.

Dressed as earlier, but with her eyes red raw from crying, was Elena. She had her arms clasped firmly in front of her blue cardigan and was chewing her back teeth angrily.

Marcello sprung off the wall as another barrage of cries filled the night air.

'If you think you can treat me with such disrespect, you better think again, young man!' she declared. 'How much did he pay you?'

Marcello was dumbstruck. Suddenly her last words filtered into his consciousness. *Pay me?*

'I asked you a question. What did that idiot give you to get you to leave me there? How much am I worth to you on the black market, then?'

Marcello's mind couldn't process the information quickly enough. 'Look, it's not as it seems. I...,' he tried, but she flared up again.

'What do you mean, *it's not as it seems?* I can assure you, it was *exactly* as it seemed! That idiot… with his hands crawling all over me...' she shuddered.

'No... Yes... what I mean is, it's not that easy. Things have been a little... well, ' he stumbled on, not really knowing how to explain the complexity of the situation; a situation that, given Elena 's point of view, was now even more complicated than he had first imagined.

She sighed. Sadness, he would have given his right arm never to see again, was welling up inside her chestnut eyes.

'Well, I hope whatever you got, it was worth it.' She turned to go back inside her house.

No!

Marcello reached out and took her gently by the arm, 'No. No, please wait. I'm sorry. I really am.'

Reacting to the softness in his voice, she took a deep breath and turned back to him.

'What went on Marcello? Why did you leave?'

Marcello looked down at his feet and exhaled. Realising there was no alternative but to explain the whole story. He looked back at her beautiful, but troubled face. 'It was the deal,' he admitted.

'…the deal? What deal?'

'The deal I had to make with Almond… if I was to get the cockerel for your father.'

Elena sighed. She looked out to sea for inspiration and then back again at Marcello. 'Look…' she pointed back towards the house, obviously too overwrought to deal with the predicament. 'I think it best if I...'

'I don't have the money to buy wonderful gifts for your father,' he blurted, knowing it was now or never. 'I knew the other boys would all bring expensive presents. Presents I could never compete with. It was my only chance of... of being with you.'

Elena started to listen closely, her face softening as he spoke.

'My only chance was the cockerel from Bellini. I sat outside your house each day and I heard how the cockerel annoyed your father every morning. The trouble was, Bellini wouldn't let me have it... not unless I could get him a bottle of the sister's liqueur.'

Elena's eyes widened.

'I persuaded the sisters to give me a bottle, but only if I got the Turkish carpet from Signora Tallocci. And then she wanted something from someone else, and so on, and so on.'

Elena was engrossed. 'Sweet Mary, and…?'

'And, the end result was, I had to do a deal with Armond.'

'And what did *he* want exactly?' she asked, her eyes narrowing with distaste.

'Well... what happened at Gianni's. Although not exactly, I'm sure,' he added, realising for the first time that his rival's evening obviously hadn't been the walk-over he'd been expecting.

Elena looked at him with a frown, trying to understand his warped thinking.

'Let me get this straight. To get the cockerel for my father, you did a deal with the whole village, ending with Armond. And, in doing so, you had to give away the only reason for doing the deals in the first place? I don't understand?'

'What? What don't you understand?' Marcello snapped, tired and frustrated.

'Why would you do such a thing? It makes no sense at all. You do all these deals and, in the end, you must give away the only reason for doing them.'

'No. Not everything.'

Elena tipped her head to one side in a desperate attempt to understand him.

Marcello looked down at the road. He scuffed the dirt with the toe of his shoe for a moment, trying to find the right words. *Just say it! What have you got to lose?*

He looked back up into her angelic face. 'Not our walk to the village; not our time at the cafe together. For just those moments, I would have made deals with the whole of Rome.'

Feeling a weight lifted off his shoulders, he sighed. It was now in the lap of the God's, he thought.

* * *

Elena looked down at the road. For a moment, like Marcello, she ran the toe of her shoe in the dirt, a million thoughts and emotions racing through her head. It was becoming difficult to even *think* straight. The memory of Marcello disappearing; that animal's hands on her knee; her running back to the house with tears in her eyes; that was anything but the date she'd so looked forward to with this complicated and passionate boy. And now, there he was, telling her a story so extraordinary that, if it wasn't for the passion in his eyes, it would be unbelievable.

She looked at the patch on the wall where he had been sitting, day in and day out, for as long as she could remember. She exhaled, letting a calm fall over her.

In the silence that followed, she realised that whatever resolve she had had dispersed. In that moment, as the warm Mediterranean breeze washed over her, she recalled the words her mother always taught her, *'Life is full of disappointments, my dear. Grab the precious moments with both hands whenever they appear.'*

She smiled and gestured to the patch of wall next to where he always sat. 'Is this seat taken?'

Marcello's eyes widened. 'Prego,' he said, stepping up to the wall and helping her up beside him.

Unsure of what to do next, they both sat in silence for a short while. As the wash of the evening waves drew out all the last of the tension in her body, Elena , realising words were of no more use, simply took Marcello's hand and placed it gently onto her lap, covering it with her own.

Melting into the warmth of his touch, they both stared out at the endless tranquil sea and watched the moonlight perform its nightly ritual, dancing upon the surface.

* * *

From an open upstairs window in the Gamboccini house, Signora Gamboccini was looking down on Marcello and Elena. She had a far away look in her eyes and, as Elena took Marcello's hand, she couldn't contain herself any longer. Pulling a white handkerchief out from her sleeve, she started to weep, uncontrollably.

Hearing the weeping from the corridor, Signor Gamboccini walked into the bedroom and appeared behind her at the window. Following her gaze, looked down at his daughter and started pointing at his wrist watch.

'What time do you call this? She should be inside!'

His wife flipped her right hand at him as if swatting an irritable mosquito, which only caused his temper to rise. She turned and pushed him across the room, giving him a warning glance.

'Hey!'

Realising no man should come between a woman and her emotions – especially when it concerned her daughter – he pottered out of the room, grunting his dissatisfaction as he went in an attempt to preserve his pride.

Turning back towards the window, and the two of them framed by the clear pale moonlight, Signora Gamboccini unrolled her handkerchief and placed it back under her nose to resume her day-dreaming. The scene reminded her of her own youth and that long lost feeling of innocence and passion her own first date had brought her... the exclusive reserve of first lovers.

SUNDAY

Another stunning summer sunrise lifted over the horizon, splashing rays of deep orange and flashes of crimson across the still ocean. Once again it promised to be a day to remember in the sleepy costal village.

Marcello and Elena were still sitting together on the wall outside the Gamboccini house, her head resting on his shoulder and both lost in each other.

Marcello, in a moment of inspiration, felt her lift her head and turn towards him. Following her lead, and the wish of every nerve in his entire body, he harmonised with her movement, lifting his eyes to gaze into hers. For one moment they just looked at each other. Then, in a moment of unity, they brought their lips together for the first time in a deep and intense kiss.

* * *

'Cwwwooookkkkkk!'

At that moment, the cockerel sat in a makeshift cage in the Gamboccini garden, started its wrangled morning crowing.

Through a half open window on the first floor of the Gamboccini house, Signor Gamboccini was fast asleep and snoring, with a satisfied grin set on his chubby face.

* * *

Suddenly, the first floor window of the neighbouring Bellini house flew open and the huge and very hung-over butcher leaned out, waving his fist in the direction of the Gamboccini's.

'Heeeyyyy!' he screamed, immediately whipping his hand up to his forehead in pain. 'Hey… *Hey, Gamboccini!* That bird, it's driving me *crazy*!'

* * *

Back in the Gamboccini bedroom, Signora Gamboccini woke with a start at the sound of Bellini's protests. She lifted her head up from the pillow and looked down at her husband, who was still in a blissful slumber. She pursed her lips together in disapproval at his petty battle with their overweight and obnoxious neighbour and gasped a sigh of resignation. Realising there were some things that would never change in this village, she dropped her head back down onto the pillow with a thump and pulled the covers back over her head. She lay there listening to the regular snoring of her husband, accompanied by the sound of Bellini's incessant ranting coming in through their open bedroom window.

'Hey… Gamboccini..! *Gamboccini! Are you listening to me?'*

* * *

Having woken at his usual time, Francesco Romero was walking through the quiet village up towards Signor Selinas's house; a small stone-built annex to the Gabriele D'Annunzio schoolhouse. It had been a long time since he had seen his beautiful village so early with anything but a thumping hangover and this morning he was enjoying the feeling of the warm morning breeze against his face and the fresh, briny smell of the harbour as if for the first time.

On his arrival at the headmaster's home, he noticed the schoolmaster's Sunday newspaper lying on the floor. Not wanting to wake him at such an early hour, Francesco picked it up and opened it out. He placed the envelope containing Marcello's essay for the University scholarship inside and then replaced the newspaper back onto the doorstep.

Striding back off towards the village, he felt a smile lift his freshly shaven cheeks. With the memory of a wonderful evening with Maria Tallocci swimming around in his head like melted chocolate and the knowledge that his son's future was secure – with, or without the help of a University scholarship – he found it hard to keep the urge to whistle at bay… and so didn't.

* * *

Up the hill at the sisters' farm, Rosetta and Leonora were enjoying their morning coffee together. Having risen to the sound of brushing, and her sister singing happily to herself downstairs as she pushed the broom back and forth across their new Turkish carpet, Leonora had made her way down the stairs in her dressing gown.

Finishing their morning cappuccino together in the winter garden, Leonora looked across at her sister.

'Oh, come on sister,' she said, with excitement. 'Let's go and have another look at Marcello's carpet.

Nodding in agreement, Rosetta helped her sister out of her wicker chair and, arm in arm, and with a youthful spring in their step, they wandered back down the hallway to admire again the restored addition to their household... courtesy of Marcello Romero.

* * *

Out in the harbour, a beautiful new speedboat was flying out across the water at full speed. Its pristine hull, crafted from the finest of woods, left a perfect white stripe in its wake across the crisp morning waters.

At the helm sat Signor Cessero. Grinning from ear to ear, his hair lifted with each leap of the boat as it hit the oncoming waves on their way out past the headland.

At the stern of the boat was Armond. Sat on the plush red leather seats and nursing a tremendous hangover, he looked decidedly worse for wear. Ignoring his father's wry smile, he looked at him as he shouted back over the sound of the engines.

'Hey, Armond, this was a great idea. Are you sure everything's OK?'

Without waiting for an answer, he gave the accelerator an extra nudge, sending the craft higher on the waves. 'At this rate, it'll only take us half an hour or so to get round to Portoforno. We should do this every weekend,' he added with a laugh.

Armond, reluctant to give his father the satisfaction of seeing him suffer, waved his approval of the idea. 'Yeah, great.'

The movement, however, was just a little too sudden. Unable to control his bodily functions any longer, he turned and threw his head over the back of the boat.

* * *

After three years of writer's block, Signora Tallocci was sitting behind her old typewriter. She had a pile of paper next to her on one side of the desk and a steaming cup of cappuccino on the other. She sat back, picked up her cup and, taking a sip of the frothy brew, let the fingers of her free hand run lovingly over the machine.

Trying to control her thoughts – an almost impossible task since the previous evening's romantic dinner with her teenage sweetheart – she replaced her cup into the saucer, took a deep breath and sat forward.

She picked up a blank piece of paper and scrolled it into the machine. Flexing her fingers, she typed something rapidly onto the middle of the paper with professional ease. Satisfied, she pulled it out of the machine and placed it down on the desk beside her, the title of her new book gazing up at her with pride:

Marcello's Date - A True story - By Maria Tallocci.

PERSONAL THANKS

To thank all the people who have influenced my life over the years would be a novel in itself. In making this list I am sure to have missed out people who have touched my life for only moments, but set off a domino effect worthy of the great Marcello Romero himself. To these I pledge my eternal thanks.

Following is a cast of the main players, so to speak, who I list (in no particular order) along with the strength which has been their highest expression of love in my life. Mere words are of no use in portraying my gratitude.

Susanne - For her purity, Dad – For his sensitivity, Mum – For her compassion, Stephen – For his inner power, John – Faith, Richard – Strength, Fiona – Care, Lynne – Love, Mike – Stability, Mick – Belief, Donna – Light heartedness, Tim – Humour, Karin – Honesty, Ben – Resolve, Damien – Openness, Steffi – Resolve, Helen – Radiance, Kevinski – Calm, Leanne – Serenity, Milli – Humour, Joy – Encouragement, Ole – Friendship, Carmen – Humour, Hazel – Thoughtfulness, Wes – Inner beauty, Linda – Warmth, Ina – Creativity, Giles – Tenderness, Britta – Freedom, Ellen – Enthusiasm, Elisabeth – Clarity, Annie – Radiance, Art – Wisdom, Wolfie – Generosity, Carmen – Tenderness, Zachi – Tenderness, Chris P. – Purity, Mary – Generosity, Ruth – Trust, Ulli – Youthfulness, Marlies – Power, Julian – integrity, Sally – Serenity, Robin – Enthusiasm, Karolin – Youthfulness, Bobby – Generosity, Marina – Belief, Allyson – Honesty, Scary – Love, Gary – Dedication, Claire – Passion, John – Warmth, Janet – Calm, Chris I. – Faith, Andrea – Humour, Douglas – Dedication, Pete – Youthfulness, Mandy – Warmth, Steve – Openness, Jude – Light heartedness, Bill – Spirit, Lynn – Fluidity, Pete – Honesty, Nigel – Solidity, Phillippa – Serenity, Dave – Ease, Bobbie – Warmth, Robert – Youthfulness, Sasha – Warmth, James – Creativity, The Keatings – Togetherness, The Kristians – Friendship, The

Laytons – Energy, Pete – Sensitivity, and especially God – For giving me all my senses and an arena in which to experience them.

I would also like to extend my thanks to Julia Cameron whose book "The Artist's Way" inspired me to give Marcello literary life and changed my own.

Lastly, I give a special thank you to my beautiful wife Susanne, without whom this book would truly never have been written

ABOUT THE AUTHOR

Mark David Hatwood spent fifteen years as a session drummer for some of the top names in the British music industry. He started his own band as songwriter in the mid 80's and, in 1991, went on to record a solo album with music legend Harald Faltermeier.

Having moved to Berlin in 1993, Mark signed a publishing deal with BMG (Bertlesmann Music Group) and went on to write music for some of the foremost European pop acts.

In 2002, Mark wrote *Marcello's Date* and has subsequently written three other screenplays and four novels including the commissioned biography of *The Scary Guy* '7 Days and 7 Nights'.

Mark currently lives and writes in Cornwall, England.